LIVERPOOL CONNECTION

About the Author

ELISABETH MARRION was born August 1948 in Hildesheim, Germany. Her father was a Corporal in the Royal Air Force and stationed after the War in the British occupied zone in Germany, where he met her mother Hilde, a war widow.

As a child Elisabeth enjoyed reading novels and plays by Oscar Wilde, Thornton Wilder and never lost her love of reading novels by Ernest Hemingway, or short stories by Guy de Maupassant.

In 1969 she moved to England, where she met her husband David. Together they established a clothing importing company. Their business gave them the opportunity to travel and work in the Sub Continent and the Far East. A large part of their working life was spent in Bangladesh, where they helped to establish a school in the rural part of the country, training young people in trades such as sign writing, electrical work and repair of computers and televisions.

For inspiration she puts on her running shoes for a long coastal run near the New Forest, where they now live.

LIVERPOOL CONNEC····· ·············TION

ELISABETH MARRION

SilverWood

Published in 2014 by the author
using SilverWood Books Empowered Publishing®

SilverWood Books Ltd
30 Queen Charlotte Street, Bristol, BS1 4HJ
www.silverwoodbooks.co.uk

ISBN 978-1-78132-229-1 (paperback)
ISBN 978-1-78132-230-7 (ebook)

British Library Cataloguing in Publication Data
A CIP catalogue record for this book is available from the British Library

Set in Sabon by SilverWood Books
Printed on responsibly sourced paper

For David

Chapter 1

Garston, Liverpool – December 1946

He crouched behind the brick wall, which was high enough for him to hide behind, but not too high to stop him from watching the comings and goings on the pavement on the opposite side of the road. From here, he had a clear view if he stood up. Behind him was a house, but he was hidden from it by a large bush. All the leaves had fallen on to the muddy floor underneath some time ago. The front garden itself was totally overgrown. Rubble from the bombed-out building next door was covered with undergrowth. You had to have your wits about you not to slip on some of the bricks, which were slippery in the damp. Yes, he had found the ideal hiding place. He knew this place well because he had come here many times before. In fact, every day this week, straight after school, not bothering to go home first.

He was shivering. His thin coat was soaked from the heavy snow, which had started to fall at lunchtime. The coat was too small for him, the sleeves riding up on his arms and no longer protecting the cracked skin on his freezing hands. A big boy had stopped him in the playground just when the teacher had turned his back to them, ready to ring the bell to let them know it was time to go back inside. He had often wondered why it was that all the children had to be outside in the cold, when the teachers were allowed to stay in the warm Principal's office drinking tea.

He had seen the big boy before and always avoided crossing his path, but he was out of luck today. The big boy put one hand on his shoulder and lifted his warm hat off his head. "Listen, squirt! If I see you near my sister again, there'll be trouble. I told her she's not allowed to play with the riff-raff from the tenements." The big boy then laughed, took the hat away with him and walked towards his mates, who had stood guard a short distance away.

"Oi! Gimme my hat back!" he shouted after them.

"You can get it back after school, outside the gate if you dare." He couldn't recall knowing the big boy's sister. She must be a girl in my class, he thought. There were about twenty girls in his class of forty-five in Year 1 at Banks Road Primary School.

By now, his feet were soaking. The cardboard in his shoes, which was in there to cover the hole in the sole, had become squishy. If he stayed here much longer, he would have to take it out. I'd be better off without it, he thought.

He raised himself up a little to take a peek over the wall, to see whether there were any left. There had been ten at the beginning of the week, but when he got here this afternoon, only three of them were still there. If he didn't do it today, his family would be the only ones in the tenement without one again.

From what he could remember, not many of them had one during the times when the bombs fell. He had vivid memories about those days. His 'old fella' and his mam would still talk about it when they thought the kids were asleep. He knew they blamed the bombs for the death of his brother, Derek, who was two years old at the time. When he had asked his Aunty Peg about it, she told him that Derek died of a fit when everybody was inside the air-raid shelter, right in the centre of Speke Road Garden. His sister, Grace, ran through burning streets to fetch the doctor, but it was too late. He was determined to provide one for the family this year. He had promised his new little brother, Alfie, and a promise is a promise.

It was time to check again, and he slowly rose from his

hiding place. Two girls brushed the snow off the wall he was hiding behind with their gloved hands. All three faced each other for a second before the first girl screamed, followed by the girl next to her, shouting, "Mam! There's somebody hiding in our front garden."

The door opened behind him, his head flew round looking towards the house. In the lit-up doorway, stood the big boy from school. In his shock, he dropped the knife, which he had taken this morning from the kitchen drawer without being seen. He had hidden it from the teachers during the day. All he could think was, Me mam will kill me if she found out I took the bread knife to school and lost it. He bent down quickly, feeling through the snow. He felt it cutting his finger, picked it up and scooted over the wall and legged it towards the wasteland before the big boy recognised him. Hearing shouts behind him, he guessed the loudest voice was the big boy's. He was now further away from the shops, and he knew if he didn't get back quickly, they would close for the evening, and then he will have missed his chance.

He crossed the road, keeping close to the wall, all the while sucking on his bleeding finger. He re-entered Vineyard Street from the other end, trying to be invisible to the men and women hurrying past him. With his back against the houses, he slowly made his way forward. Just like his hero, Roy Rogers, in the cinema. His Aunty Flo had given him a ticket to see a film on his last birthday. He had planned to mingle with the shoppers, take it and leave. With all his running around, it was getting late, and there were only one or two people around. He could see the owner inside at the till. This was it. He took the knife and reached up as high as he could to cut the top off. He had to have several goes, but his efforts were rewarded. The top of the tree fell to the ground, at least two feet, he imagined. Just then, there were shouts from inside the shop. The owner had seen him.

"Stop! Stop that boy!"

But David had learned to be fast. Despite the weight and the prickly branches, he made off. He was cunning, in spite of his young age. He ran in a different direction to his home, back to the wasteland. He pulled his trophy behind him up the hill. All he needed to do was slide down on all fours to the other side. From there he would crawl through the hole in the wire fence. He felt his coat being caught on a piece of wire, which he should have remembered. They had put it there themselves to stop others from finding the treasure, which they kept hidden under the largest tree. They had dug themselves a really big hole, using only branches and their bare hands when the ground was still soft. He smiled at the memory of that day. He gave a pull and heard his coat rip. He tried to see the damage. This was supposed to be for Alfie when he gets bigger, he thought. He looked at his snow-covered tree. Like the picture in a book, he had seen in a library. The same book, which was hidden under his bed. If only it would stay that way, there would be no need to decorate it.

Chapter 2

"Annie! Wait!" Annie was loading the half-dry washing back into the pram. She had been at the wash house all afternoon. She worried about getting home late, arriving after George got back cold and hungry from work. You never knew what mood he would be in. He wanted the tin bath to be ready for him in front of the fire as soon as he stepped through the door. She also needed to hurry and check on her youngest. Our Alfie reminds me so much of Derek, she thought every time she looked at him. Alfie was fast approaching the same age Derek had been when he was so cruelly taken from her that night at the air-raid shelter. Annie had left Dorothy at home from school today to look after him. She would also have to go to the grocery shop in Vineyard Street. It was only Wednesday and already the money George had given her to last till Friday had been spent. There was no point asking him for an advance this early in the week. Dorothy would have to persuade Joel Brown to let them have some bread, eggs and milk 'on tick'. The same at the butcher's for a ham bone and some dripping.

They could have ham and pea soup tomorrow. But Annie had no idea what she would serve for dinner tonight. Dorothy didn't like going to the shop. A boy there called her 'Bloody Irish' every time she went in. Annie would have to have a word the next time she saw him. She hoped Dorothy wouldn't forget to pick up the medicine for her dad, which was ready for them at the chemist and not leave the ration book behind like last time. "Annie! Wait!" Her friend Flo had caught up with her. Flo had found work again at the wash house. Ironic really, her working here again. She opened up first thing in the morning, just before the caretaker would arrive. The two would light the large boilers, which heated the water. Flo also helped with collecting the money. The amount was set by how much washing you brought in. There were large scales for weighing your 'dirties'. Most women would come here once a fortnight with smaller loads, carrying their laundry in heavy looking baskets or in old pillowcases. Annie often wondered how some of them could afford it.

Annie barely had enough money to come here every three weeks. The smaller pieces of washing she would do in the sink at home, or boil a pan on the stove, but she kept her larger pieces for a visit to the wash house. It was quite a journey pushing the pram, especially in the winter when she added some towels. "It is easier to dry them there, rather than in the front room before the fire," she would argue with George. George would get mad at her when he came home, and the washed nappies were still over the wooden rack. I hope Dorothy remembers to take them down.

But Annie would not want to miss her visits to the wash house. Here, she met her neighbours for the latest gossip and news. Anyway, with Flo in charge, Annie's wash would not get weighed. Flo simply wrote in the ledger, 'Annie owes 6d'. They kept quiet about it, of course. The little bit Annie sometimes managed to save, she kept in her special box at home. She knew nobody ever touched it. Annie believed John, the caretaker, knew what Flo was doing. But Flo seemed to have a very close relationship with him. Annie suspected there was more to it than Flo let on. She would be happy for her friend, after everything she went through.

"No need to hurry, Annie!" shouted a woman from the sink next to the one Annie had used.

"He'll be fast asleep by the time you get back. They worked our men really hard today. My Paul hardly managed to crawl up the staircase, that's how tired he was."

"I wonder whether any of our old fellas made it home tonight. Have you seen the snowstorm?" added another neighbour just entering. "So, you have one after all," she continued, looking at Annie.

"One of what? What do you mean, Marge?" Annie had stopped in her tracks.

"A Christmas tree. I just saw your David carrying it up the stairs."

"A Christmas tree? Are you sure it was our David?"

"Sure, I am sure. I know your David, don't I?"

"I'd better hurry, Flo." Annie started coughing, looking at her friend.

"Wait! Somebody left a scarf last week, I'll get it."

And she was gone, returning a few minutes later.

"What if that woman remembers and sees me wearing it?"

"Annie, look at it. It's grey wool. Now look at everyone here. How many grey scarves can you see? They all have one, right? Besides, the woman can afford to lose it. I removed the label with her name on it," she whispered, and then laughed out loud.

Chapter 3

Annie could hear shouting as soon as she opened the door at the entry of the tenement block. Their apartment was on the third floor at Speke Road Garden. It had taken her longer than usual to push the pram up the hill through the snow. She nearly fell over twice, that's how slippery it was. She never gave her lack of strength and her prolonged coughing fits a second thought these days. For the last few yards, she'd found it easier to pull the pram behind her instead of pushing it. That way, she could push against the entrance door with her back. The door always stuck when it was damp. Freddy, David's mate, who lived in the tenement opposite, came jumping down, taking several steps at one time.

"Evening," he said when he shot past her. Several neighbours had come out of their flats, standing grouped together talking. Some were straining their necks to see whether they could spot where the commotion came from. Annie stood there, frozen to the spot. The pram with the washing was still outside in the snow.

"Give Annie a hand with her washing. Don't just gawk at her," one of the neighbours shouted at a boy slightly older than David.

"Why me? She has enough of her own brood upstairs to help her." He made a movement with his head indicating above.

"Because I'll clout you if you don't, that's why."

The neighbour had walked over to where Annie stood, and her son reluctantly followed. Both women took the washing from the pram, each carrying about half the load.

The boy lifted the pram.

"Bloody hell, Mam," He exclaimed, surprised at how heavy it was.

"Oi! Watch your mouth, otherwise, I'll have a word with your dad!"

"But it's really heavy. What have you got in there?" He looked up at Annie, who by now had reached the third floor.

She had to stop twice to catch her breath before she got to her front door. The shouting was louder up here. The boy dropped the pram and ran back downstairs, not wanting to get any more instructions. His mam placed the washing she had carried up back into it. She then took Annie's from her arms and placed it on top.

"Call me if you need any help."

Dorothy was standing inside the hallway with a bucket of coal she had just taken from the storage cupboard.

"Is your dad back?" Annie asked.

Dorothy looked slightly guilty.

"Did you get the medicine?"

"I forgot."

"Dorothy!"

"Mam, I can't do everything around here, you should have been home." With that, Dorothy walked into the kitchen, not waiting for her mother. But not before she muttered, "I should have never come back." Hoping her mother did not hear that.

"You are late!" George shouted as soon as he saw Annie entering the kitchen.

Annie looked at George, pearls of sweat running from his forehead. Annie knew he had not fully recovered, and felt guilty she had begged him to go back to work. "How is your fever?"

"Bloody awful," George was shivering and put his hands towards his face, trying to mop his forehead with the handkerchief he had pulled out of his work trousers.

"Dorothy, put your coat on and run to the chemist. Kick their back door in if you have to, but get the medicine."

"But, Mam!"

"Dorothy, hurry up."

"I'll go." David stood up and walked towards his mother.

"Oh, no, you don't. I think I have to have a word with you, young man." She took a minute to look at David, George temporarily forgotten.

"Why are you bleeding? And why are your trousers ripped? What have you been up to? Come over here."

David slowly walked towards his mam. Before David had a chance to reply, they heard banging against the door.

"We haven't finished." Annie turned around, went back to the hall and opened the door. A woman she had seen before, but could not place, stood next to the owner of the greengrocer's.

"Your son stole a Christmas tree from outside my shop. Cut the top right off. I want you to pay for it, and here, you can have the rest of the tree." He threw the remainder of the tree inside.

"David, come here." David slowly walked over and hid behind his mother.

"Did you hear what Mr Smith just said?"

"Yes, Mam."

"Do you have a Christmas tree?"

"Yes, Mam."

"Where did you get it from?"

"Found it."

"You found it?" Now it was Mr Smith asking the questions. "But this woman here, she saw you cutting it off and taking it."

"She actually saw it was my David?"

"No, it was too dark, but it was a boy, looking very much like him."

"Mam, what's going on?" Jeffrey, returning from work, appeared behind the shop owner.

"This woman is accusing our David of stealing a Christmas tree."

"David, do you have a Christmas tree?"

"Yes."

"Where did you get it from?"

"Found it."

"There you are. You heard the lad – he found it. Now bugger off." With that, Jeffrey entered the flat and shut the door in the greengrocer's face.

Chapter 4

"Did you get a hiding for it?" Freddy was sitting at the edge of the water, dangling his feet into it. "Blimey, that's freezing!"

"What?"

"Did you get a hiding for it? The Christmas tree?"

"No, me dad wasn't well that night, and later on he couldn't be bothered." David opened the door of the changing room and came to sit next to his friend and tested the water himself, slowly dipping his left foot in.

"Bloody hell. It's cold!" He turned his head, trying to spot his older brother, Jeffrey, who had let them in for free. He was a Garston Baths lifeguard, but typically, Jeffrey was nowhere to be seen. "See me brother anywhere?" Freddy pointed towards a dim corner at the end of the pool where young Jeffrey was chatting to a girl. She had her back to them, but David thought she must have just come out of the water. She looked freezing. Her arms were wrapped around her, and water was dripping off the blue striped swimming costume. Jeffrey turned his head, spotted David and waved for him to come over.

"What?" David noticed who the girl standing with his brother was. She worked at the paper shop on Saturdays, the one near the wasteland. He was not allowed to play there, and if his old man found out about it, there would be trouble. It was a place where people had started to dump some of their household rubbish. He and his mates would sneak through the hole in the fence and get their large sticks, which were hidden beneath some bushes. They would poke through the rubbish and pick up everything worth keeping, but what they were really after were empty beer or pop bottles. Occasionally, they found one or two. They would give them a quick clean with their sweaters, and run to the local off-licence, taking turns on who would go in. The geezer there could be really grumpy sometimes, and it didn't help that he was teased by most boys in the street because of the way he walked. David's mum had told him off once, when she caught him making fun of him behind his back. "Me dad wants his money for the empties," one of the boys would say, handing over the bottles.

"How much did you get?"

"A farthing."

"That's not enough."

"It's all I got."

"The bloke's cheating on us, he knows it's not your old man who sent you."

"Well, it's all we got."

"Who's going in?"

"I'll go." It was usually David who volunteered to go inside the paper shop. He liked the colourful displays and the sweet smells. But best of all, if there were other customers being served, nobody would notice if you helped yourself to a packet of pretend cigarettes, which were kept close to the front door. Unfortunately for him, most of the time, they heard you entering since the door had a tendency to stick, and you had to hit it hard with your shoulder. He approached the counter, used his best smile, looked up at the girl, pointed to the jars behind her and said, "Two Black Jacks."

"How much money have you got?" He held out his hand.

"Did you bring your ration book?"

"Me mam's taken it to work."

"I can't give you any then." When he turned around to leave, she said, "Wait, I'll give you one, but don't tell on me." Proudly, he presented the sweet to his mates. "I got it, so I'm having the first lick."

Now, the same girl who gave him his sweets looked at him closely and asked, "Don't I know you from somewhere?"

"Me? No, never seen you before." David hoped that would get her off his back. "Rita, this is my little brother, David." Jeffrey grabbed David by the arm before he could disappear.

"Now I remember," Rita said.

"No, you don't." Now Freddy had joined the small gathering at the edge of the swimming pool.

"Yes, I do. You're both in the same class as my little sister."

Both David and Freddy's mouths dropped open. As if on cue, they both asked, "Who is your sister?"

"Carol. You know her. We live in Vineyard Street. I live there with me mam, brother and sister, opposite the greengrocer."

Chapter 5

"'Oh, Danny Boy, the pipes, the pipes are calling. From glen to glen, and down the mountain side. The summer's gone, and all the roses are falling. It's you, it's you must go, and I must bide'." Annie was singing to herself, which she did often when she was alone. Today was an especially difficult day. She had finally taken the small suitcase from underneath the bed. The little brown one with two spring locks, both of them now slightly rusty from the constant damp in the apartment caused by the winter fog.

She detected a slight tremor in her hands as she touched the case, bent down and blew the dust away. Then she stroked it and felt the roughness of the leather with a sad look in her eyes. She would not be able to do this, unless she was on her own. She could not touch the case if George was here. He knew she still blamed him for Derek's death that night in the dark shelter. Every time after that, when the sirens went off at night, it was Annie who was out of bed first, hurrying to where the children were sleeping and shook them awake. Not bothering waking George. In total silence, the older kids quickly helped to get the little ones dressed, grab their gas masks and run down the staircase, out of the front door and find a place inside the bomb shelter, which was located in the middle of the Speke Road Garden tenements.

Annie was the last to leave. George previously refused to go, always saying, "No, I'm sure that was 'the all clear', go back to bed, woman!" He would turn over and continue snoring. Some of the nights she had not enough time to dress her baby and took him as he was, just wrapped in a blanket.

She had become numb to the noises of arriving aircrafts, of bombs hitting the ground, of explosions around her and the heat of the blazing fires. She no longer turned round to check whether the match works got a hit again. Just rushed after her children.

"Get a doctor!" Grace running off, forgetting the dangers outside, was all she remembered of the night little Derek died in the air-raid shelter. She knew Flo had arrived at the apartment soon after. She told her so. She found Annie in bed with Derek's body and no sign of George.

I must to do it today, thought Annie. I doubt if I'll find the strength again. Click, both locks opened at once. The smell of mothballs, which she had carefully placed under the top layer of tissue paper, hit her nose. She recoiled and for a brief second, was tempted to close it again. She let out a sigh and lifted the paper. It's just as I left it. What else did she expect to see? Annie picked up the first item with both hands, a light blue cardigan that would fit Alfie perfectly, plus the trousers and socks she now took out. Annie lifted them to her face and searched for a familiar smell. But all traces of Derek had been taken away. Soon, he will just be a distant memory. She cried at that thought. No, she was determined Derek would always remain with her. The baby boots, which she had kept, together with his dummy, were in her wooden box at her bedside table and every so often, when George was out, she would get them out, hold them close and picture Derek. Instead of mothballs, those items still smelled of him.

Chapter 6

Ballyshannon, Ireland – Spring 1926

"You can be a very determined young lady, Annie." Her mother was checking the stew, which was on the stove, almost ready to be served. "What makes you think it's better over there? Wait until your father hears about it. He fought for our freedom here, and it's bad enough the others have already deserted us, and now you as well."

"Our Paddy isn't leaving, and both our Peg and our Kate have settled well over there, and I can live with one of them. Both told us there is plenty of work. Tell me honestly, Mam, do you not rely on the money they keep sending us? Their money, which puts food on this table. Our father's not much help, is he? No, but the local pub profits are booming." Annie finished the last sentence quietly, no point of rubbing it in anymore.

"Now don't you be disrespectful of your dad, young Annie, he does his best, and you know as well as I do, as soon as you have left, our Paddy, when he is old enough, will be off as well."

"Mam, there's no work here, the yarn and textile mills are too far away, plus nobody else is hiring. I've made up my mind. We're leaving next week, Flo and I. We're going together." Flo and Annie had started to plan their journey to Liverpool several weeks ago. First, it was just a crazy thought. Both of them were looking for work, without success. The queues at the labour exchange grew longer every day. They listened to disgruntled voices whilst waiting in line. One woman behind them had said,

"My cousin went to England, she now has a good job at a department store in Liverpool. I don't know why we're not all going over there. Separate country or not, I need to feed my children."

Annie and Flo looked at each other. "No good standing here in line at the dole office, if we are going to work in England, is there?" Flo finally found her voice, and without a second thought, they left the queue and started planning there and then.

Annie's mother had no idea that Peg had loaned her the money for the ferry, and once they reached Dublin, they would stay with Flo's aunt and uncle until they managed to get a crossing. Mother Superior strictly forbade them such a move! Only immoral women or Protestants would entertain such improper ideas. She persuaded Father O'Connor to come over to the house, to give the girls a good talking to. However, Annie's dad had lost all respect for the Father two years before, when he had begged him to allow his youngest to be buried at the local cemetery, although she had not yet been christened.

"No chance that we will get the papers, which would allow us to go by train." Flo looked at Annie whilst they were making a list of the few things they would be taking with them.

"Anyway, my dad wouldn't let me apply for a pass through Northern Ireland to go from one end of our own country to the other just to reach Dublin. 'It's a bloody disgrace and principles are principles,' he said."

"So how are we supposed to get there, Flo?"

"Easy, I know a bloke who has a lorry, and he goes back and forth to Dublin. I can ask him whether he can give us a lift."

"A lorry? All the way to Dublin? What is he doing there?"

"Annie, I have no idea. All I know is he takes things to the harbour. Now, do we want to go to Dublin or not?"

Annie nodded in agreement. "It's a long way to go by lorry, mind you."

"And Annie, for God's sake, don't ask him what he does. I can imagine it's not strictly legal. Promise me."

"Flo, you are not getting us arrested, are you?"

"Now you are being daft, Annie."

Young Paddy carried Annie's case to the place where the girls had agreed to meet the driver. "Annie, when I'm bigger can I come, too?" He looked at her with his big dark brown pleading eyes, eyes which seemed too large for his small pale face.

"Of course, Paddy, I will be waiting for you, you hear." With that, she gave him a hug, something she had never done before. "Now, you run back home before it gets dark. Please don't look back, she thought, otherwise I might change my mind, but the lorry was in sight and Flo told her to hurry up. The man opening the driver's side door could not have been much older than Annie or Flo. Surely he was not the driver? Annie strained her neck to see up and through the open passenger window. Two more faces looked down in her direction.

"There are already people sitting there, Flo." Annie was now worried that they may have been conned, that there was no lift to Dublin after all, and she would have to go back home and face her mother.

"Come on, you two, don't just stand there, we don't have all day. I hope you have your shilling ready," the driver said, looking from Flo to Annie.

"Where do you want us to sit?" Annie asked.

"Up there." Only now she realised there were more people at the back on the top of the open lorry. Before she had time to consider, she handed over her shilling, was helped up and joined a noisy group of men and women. Mentally, she counted her remaining money: the fare her sister sent her, plus her mother had given her an Irish Punt and her father a further ten shillings. How they managed that, she would always wonder.

"'Oh Danny boy, the pipes, the pipes are calling. From glen to glen, and down the mountain side. The summer's gone, and all the roses are falling. It's you, It's you must go, and I must bide'."

Chapter 7

Tired and exhausted, Annie and her best friend, Flo, arrived in Liverpool one week after they had first set foot on to the top of the lorry. Tired but in high spirits. High spirits. Just thinking about another drink made Annie feel sick. There should have been enough room at the top of the lorry for about eight people, but when Annie and Flo climbed up to find a place to sit, about twenty people moved closer together to make some space.

"Hope he doesn't make many more stops," sighed a young chap who moved over to make room for Flo. "On second thought, if on all of the stops more young beauties like you join us, there will be space on my lap, I say!"

"You wash your mouth out, young man. Has your mam not told you how to greet a lady proper?" Flo replied and squeezed between him and Annie.

"Pardon me for forgetting me manners, Miss. My name is Kieran and with whom do I have the honour?" He stood up, took a bow, stretched his hand out to greet her at the same moment as the lorry started to move forward, and he lost his balance.

"Wow! Are all the young men this forward where you come from?" replied Flo.

His face was so close to hers; she felt his warm breath on her cheeks and pushed him away. The lorry made a left turn and Kieran tumbled backwards, ending up on the knees of a fellow passenger, who stood up. Judging from his frame, he must have come from a family of giants.

"Oi! Watch it!"

"I'm sorry, really, mate." Kieran was now totally flustered; his face was bright red, his eyes towards the floor, his cockiness momentarily deserting him.

"Come back over here, Kieran. I'm Flo, and this is my friend, Annie."

Flo stood up, held her skirt on each side with her hands, curtsied and said, "Pleased to meet you, Kieran."

The rest of the group had turned quiet during their exchange, but now lost interest and continued with their rowdy chatter. A woman next to Annie handed her a bottle.

"What's in there?"

"Courage, Annie – there, take a sip." Annie took the bottle and recoiled at the strong smell, but, determined not to be shown up, put it towards her lips and took a swig. The strong liquid burned her throat. She bent over and started coughing but passed it on to Flo.

"What have you got there?"

"I believe it's called courage, Flo. I think we could definitely do with some." She started giggling. Flo took a big gulp.

"Jesus! That's brilliant, where is that coming from?" A dozen hands pointed to the other end of the lorry where several wooden crates were stuck about six feet high. From the height and the width, she reckoned, at least twenty crates. "Shall there never be a dull moment in our life," she laughed and raised the bottle again.

Kieran was woken by rough hands shaking him on his shoulder. "That's it, folks, this is as far as I take you. You're on your own from here on. And good luck." The driver jumped off the back. Their fellow passengers where already standing at the roadside.

"Where are we?"

"East gate. You better hurry down, mate. I can't linger here. It's light soon. Reach those cases down, will you?"

Kieran joined Annie and Flo who were gathering their belongings.

"Now what?"

"Now what, what?" asked Flo in return.

"Well, I mean it's too early for the ticket office and to secure a place in the queue. We should find a cafe and blow sixpence on a sturdy breakfast." He felt safer directing his speech to Annie. He had already worked out that Flo was a force to be reckoned with.

"Kieran, I don't want to know what your plans are, but we are off to find my aunt and uncle, and no, you are not coming along," Flo added quickly.

"I can wait outside their place for you, or you could tell them I am your cousin, being sent along to keep an eye on you two, or..." But Flo stopped him there.

"Don't be daft, they would know all my cousins."

"I could be Annie's cousin. Yes, that makes sense. Surely, Annie, you do have a cousin Kieran, have you not?"

Annie, who was recovering slowly from feeling slightly queasy from all the drinks they consumed during the night had to laugh.

"Actually, I do have a cousin Kieran."

"There you have it, Flo, how could you leave the cousin of your best friend all alone at the docks and without breakfast."

Kieran now smiled his best charmed smile ever.

"My uncle will kill me, but I wasn't to know that Annie would bring her cousin. Shame on you, Annie. Kieran, you might as well take our cases. No point having a man along otherwise, is there?"

Chapter 8

The girls in front, arms linked, and giggling, were carrying only their small bags over their shoulders. They could hear Kieran huffing and puffing behind them, struggling with the three cases. They reached Parnell Street about forty-five minutes after they set off. Kieran had stopped several times, put the cases down, trying to catch his breath.

"Girls! Girls! Wait for me!" Kieran tried his best to keep up. "Can you take at least one case for a while?" he begged.

"But, cousin! Surely, no cousin of ours would suggest we do the heavy work. Would they, Annie? Anyway, it's not much further, stop complaining."

"Tell me your aunt and uncle live on the bottom floor," Kieran said, standing in front of the red brick built tenement block. He was raising his head to count the number of floors, just in case the answer was, as he fully expected it to be, a no.

"You are out of luck, cousin. Don't worry, it's not all the way up – just to the fourth floor. On second thoughts, you stay down here. We don't want my aunt to keel over in shock, if we arrive with a total stranger in tow. Annie, your cousin is a pain, anyway." She looked at a worried Kieran who realised with some relief that she was smiling at him.

Kieran sat on one of the suitcases outside the entrance after Flo and Annie disappeared through the door. Jesus, he thought, as far as you can see, brick built building after brick built building. It was not yet seven o'clock in the morning and already the street was getting busy. An urchin played in the street, kicking an old tin can in front of him. A woman came through the door pushing a pram. Kieran jumped up and helped her down the rest of the stairs.

"My, we have a real gentleman here. Well thank you, young man," she said and went on her way.

"Who are you and why are you loitering around here? Whose cases are those? Have you been stealing, lad?" Came a gruff male voice.

Before he found words to reply, a skinny young boy came through the entrance and squeezed himself between the man and Kieran.

"You Annie's cousin?" the boy asked. Kieran nodded, relieved. "Me mam sent me to give you a hand." With that, he bent down and took what looked to him to be the smallest of the three cases.

"See, I am Annie's cousin," Kieran said to the man, who still had not moved. He took one suitcase with each hand and pushed past him after the boy.

Flo's aunt greeted him with welcoming open arms and hugged him tight. "I'm so glad somebody had some sense and didn't let those two girls travel all the way to England on their own. You take good care of them, you hear?"

"Is that bacon I can smell?"

"Put all your things over there, sit yourselves down. I'll get you a good breakfast. After that, you'll have to get down to the docks quickly, and get in line for your papers to be stamped, and then wait in another queue to get the tickets for a crossing. My Aiden says the line is getting longer every day, and it might take several days until you're seen. You might not even get a crossing to Liverpool, but to somewhere totally different instead."

"But my sister is waiting for me in Liverpool." Annie realised for the first time that it was not going to be as straightforward as she had imagined.

"You lot had better be going as fast as you can, and Kieran, don't let these two out of your sight. There are some unsavoury characters down at the docks."

"No, I won't, Missus O'Finnigan. You can rely on cousin Kieran," he said with a mouth full of bread with crispy bacon. He tried to ignore the daggers being shot from Flo's eyes in his direction.

Chapter 9

"Will I be glad when we finally reach land," Annie managed to say before she was seasick again. The three of them eventually managed to get on a ferry from Dublin to Holyhead a few days after they arrived at Flo's aunt and uncle's place. Each morning before the sun was up, they were ready in the queue, waiting in line to be seen. On the third day of waiting, they were finally interviewed by the English administration office and quizzed about their plans and who they would be living with. They kept the story of Kieran being Annie's cousin alive, fearing he would not get the required papers and be declined a ferry ticket. He had already confessed to them, that without Annie's sister, he had no address to go to.

"If we carry on like that, I may start believing you are my cousin after all."

The Curraghmore had set sail at 05.30 in the morning. Flo's aunt and uncle used the neighbour's pram for the transport of their cases and came along to wave goodbye.

They were greeted by total chaos at the dockside. Annie, Flo and Kieran almost turned round to go back home. But Flo's uncle was going to have none of that. He pushed them through the crowds using the pram as a weapon. This was his workplace, and he was in his dockworker's overalls, which gave him a look of authority and an advantage for his young charges.

"Make some space, matey," he said to a sturdy fellow at the front of the line. All the while people were pushing and shouting. Annie got elbowed in her side during a shuffle.

She keeled over and stumbled forward, but that motion propelled her several spaces ahead of the others.

"Oi, we are with her, let us through." Kieran reacted with speed, took the first suitcase and handed it to Annie. Ignoring everybody around him, he grabbed Flo's arm and pushed her towards where Annie was now standing. Swiftly, he handed her a case, took his own and kicked the fellah in front who shot round. Kieran shrugged his shoulders and said, "Real sorry, mate. See me dad over there? He told me to keep an eye on me sisters."

Flo's uncle had now been joined by two of his pals, one of them, a real sturdy fellow towering over the crowd. The guy Kieran had kicked immediately calmed down. Flo's family waved the three of them on and nodded encouragingly.

"Kieran, do you have to unpack the sandwiches right now?" Annie felt her stomach turning again.

"A man needs his strength, especially heaving your two cases around." He continued to inspect what Flo's aunt had packed for them to eat on the way.

"Put them down. We can at least wait until we are on the train," Flo now intervened, anything was better than Annie being sick again.

The crossing took several hours and Annie, Flo and Kieran hardly ever left the seats they found, in the fear that the people sitting on the floors around them would get up and claim them as theirs. Annie being sick in a bucket a steward had given her, ensured a little space around them. Assumingly, nobody wanted to arrive in England with somebody else's puke on their clothes. A green looking Annie, a happy looking Flo and a boisterous Kieran disembarked late afternoon and set foot on dry land at the dockside in Holyhead. It took a further two hours until they were processed to carry on.

"You two wait here, I will try to get our train tickets

and find out where we have to go," Kieran volunteered. "How much money have you left?"

"Kieran, you are not planning to run off with our money, are you?"

"Now, would I cheat on my own family, Flo?" He put his best hurt face on when he looked at her.

"Well, the crossing was seven shillings and the train can't be more than two shillings each, surely. Here, we'll both give you three shillings. You too, Kieran, show us your money. Now this should be more than enough," Flo continued.

"Do you think we can trust him?" Annie asked after Kieran left.

"If not, I'll make it my personal mission to hunt him down. You have my word on that," Flo replied.

Beaming, Kieran was back within twenty minutes, grinning from ear to ear. "The train leaves in half an hour, we have to change trains in Chester and from there to Liverpool Lime Street Station. Oh, yes, and here is your change. It was one shilling and six pence each. There, as I said, you can rely on cousin Kieran."

They had to stand on the train all the way to Chester, but they let Annie sit on the suitcases. She still looked a little pale.

"What are we going to do when we get to Liverpool?" Kieran asked after the third bite into Flo's aunt's sandwiches.

"What are *we* going to do? I tell you what, Kieran, I have no idea what you are going to do, but I know what Annie and I are going to do. Annie here, she is going to her sister, Peg, in Allerton and me – who actually does have a cousin Maureen, who has a market stall at the Garston market – is where I am going to live and work. You, however, Kieran, have no idea where to go."

"This cousin of yours, she has a husband?"

"Yes, and he works at the Garston docks."

"Garston has a dock?" She saw Kieran's face brighten up when he said it. "Oh, no," she moaned, "don't even think about it."

"Hand on me heart, I promised your aunt and uncle not to let you out of my sight." As far as Kieran was concerned, that was it.

"Jesus, Kieran, how did we end up with you, of all the good looking fellas on that lorry?" All three of them looked at each other and burst out laughing.

They found three seats on the train from Chester to Liverpool Lime Street Station. Annie was perking up when they let her have the seat by the window, and she ignored the others when the train set off. Once the train had gathered speed, the steam from the engine was dissipated by the wind, and Annie could take in everything she saw on the way. It was beginning to get dark outside, but Annie kept her face pressed onto the window. Not much different from home, she thought, until the lights of Liverpool appeared in the distance. "Look, look over there, Liverpool!" An excited Annie jumped up and made space for her friends.

Chapter 10

"Annie, Jesus, what were you thinking?" Peg was still shaking her head.

"We could not just leave him behind, could we now? Actually, it was pretty useful having Kieran around. I don't think we could have managed without him, and Flo's aunt and uncle trusted him," Annie replied.

"Of course they trusted him. He is *your cousin*, after all."

When Peg had opened the door after ten o'clock that night, she did not recognise the three strangers in front of her straight away. The street lights were out again. Nobody had bothered fixing them this time. All Peg could make out were three figures huddling in the shadows. She quickly tried to shut the door, but Kieran put his foot into the entrance so the door could not close completely. "What do you think you are doing?" shouted Peg. "Who is it?" they heard Bob's voice asking from inside the house. "Peg, it's me, Annie."

"Oh, my God, Annie!" Now her hands flew across her mouth. "What are you doing here?"

"What am I doing here? Have you forgotten? You sent me the money for the fare. Didn't you get my letter? I wrote to you that I was coming. How about letting us in?" Annie was getting embarrassed in front of her friends.

Now Bob had appeared to check what was going on. "Annie?"

At last, they were all sitting around the kitchen table. Annie had made the introductions, and Peg had made a pot of tea and cut big pieces of bread and covered it with margarine and some cheese. Kieran decided his best policy was to keep quiet. He could feel the tension between Annie and her sister. He concentrated on eating as much as he was allowed to. Peg's husband, Bob, never let him out of his sight, scrutinising him suspiciously.

Flo thought she might as well act like it was the most normal thing that Annie and she arrived late at night with a total stranger in tow. She chipped in when Annie told them the whole trip from the beginning and made it sound like it was all her idea to ask Kieran along.

It was impressive how convincing Annie sounded when she implied that Kieran had been a friend from the social club they used to go to, and the three of them decided to go to Liverpool together. Flo kicked Kieran under the table to make sure he was listening.

"Ouch."

"Sorry, Kieran, give me a bit of space will you?"

Peg got an extra blanket and pillow from a cupboard and made Kieran a bed in the front room. Flo went off to the spare room she would share with Annie. Bob had to leave for work, but not before giving Annie a big hug and shaking his head he said, "Well, welcome, Annie, why do I get the feeling there are going to be challenging times ahead?" Annie and Peg wanted to stay up a little bit longer. Peg wanted to hear all the news from home and Annie wanted to tell about her adventure again and again. She told Peg about Liverpool Lime Street Station. The imposing glass ceiling, the forbidding looking dark wooden panelling. How they had to go to Pier Head to take the number 49 tram, change at Penny Lane and finally reached Peg's house. How she had felt just like Little Orphan Annie, her nickname given to her by Peg after the play the nuns made them put on every year. Annie temporarily forgetting that Peg had lived in Liverpool for the last few years and must know her way around. Finally, she took a deep breath, sighed and said,

"Look, Peg, Flo is off to her cousin's in the morning, she lives in Campania Street. If Flo and I find work soon, we could rent a room there, and I would be out of your way."

"Now you are being silly, Annie. No need to sulk. You will stay here, of course. Our mam would kill us if I let you live by yourself at only sixteen."

"I will pay my way as soon as I have a job. Did you ask the foreman at the bottle works whether there is a job for me?"

"Yes, and he made it perfectly clear, they are not hiring at the moment. There is talk about a General Strike next month, organised by the Trade Unions." Annie's face fell as her sister spoke.

"But since you are my sister, I am supposed to bring you along as soon as you get here." Peg beamed when she finished her sentence.

Chapter 11

The next morning Annie found a note on the kitchen table:

Annie, have gone to work, will tell the foreman you have arrived. Bob still sleeping, don't disturb, he's doing nightshift for the rest of the week. Flo and Kieran can keep their stuff here until they have sorted themselves out. There is bread and cheese in the larder. Use the milk, don't want it to go off, but go to the shops round the corner and buy new one for Bob.
    See you later, kiss, Peg.

Annie was relieved that the note sounded much more relaxed than the conversation they had about Annie's new found friend the night before.

"Did Peg get you a job at the bottle works?" asked Flo, still holding Peg's note in her hand.

"They said they are really not hiring anybody right now, but to bring me along. That sounds promising, don't you think?"

"Yes, definitely," said Kieran, still sleepy, followed by, "What's the plan for today?"

"Kieran, you are too much, you are, get yourself off the chair and let's go. We don't want to use the hospitality of Annie's sister longer then we need to, come on."

"Where to?"

"We'll go to my cousin's house, and if she is not there, check with a neighbour, maybe somebody will know where she works."

"I thought she has a market stall?"

"She has, but today is not Saturday, is it? She only does that on Saturdays."

"Who do we say I am, when your cousin asks?"

"Well, you are Annie's cousin, of course."

"But why don't I live here where my cousins live?"

"Because you are a nuisance and they kicked you out. That is why. Come on, let's go."

"What will you do, Annie?" Flo turned round to face her.

"I think I should spend some of my money and get everything for a great Irish stew, and cook it, so when my sister comes back, the dinner is ready, and Bob can have some before he goes off to work. Do you think that's a good idea?"

"That is a bloody good idea," said Kieran, who had perked up at the sound of food.

"Yes, don't worry I will make enough for all of us. You just concentrate on finding work and lodgings." She pushed them out of the door and closed it behind them.

"That was great, Annie," Peg admitted when everybody sat round the table later in the evening.

"It almost brings tears to my eyes. I have not tasted a good Irish stew since our mam made it last time I was at home. Thank you, Annie, that was really thoughtful of you."

"Annie, get a bottle of beer." Peg looked at Kieran and smiled. "Annie, get two bottles of beer, lucky you thought of buying some today. Kate will be coming very soon."

"Does your sister, Kate, live nearby?" asked Flo.

"No, she lives all the way over in Birkenhead. She will stay over tonight, she can sleep with me. Good job that Bob is on nightshift." Now they all laughed.

"Did he really say I could start at the bottle works on

43

Monday?" Annie asked Peg for the third time that evening.

"Yes, and you'd better work hard. Otherwise, he'll kill me."

"What about you, Flo, how did you get on?" asked Peg.

"Well, we went to my cousin's house, and she was not there. We found a neighbour who told us my cousin works at the match works, you know, the one in Speke Road. I went there, and they let me wait until lunch break. Somebody found her for me, and she came back and gave me her keys. I asked her whether there was any work there and she said she would ask. Tonight, when she came home, she said there was none because everybody is worried that there will be a national strike, but they kept a note of my name."

"What will you do?"

"I am moving to my cousin's in the morning, thank you for letting me stay, Peg. I will look for work, and in the meantime, my cousin said I can help at the wash house. She knows the woman who runs it, and they always need extra hands. Then there is the market stall, I will work at. I will be fine, next time I come and visit you, I will be a proper employed lady."

Kieran had been quiet throughout the banter, drinking his beer, deep in thought.

"And young Kieran," said Peg. "What sort of day did my young *cousin* have?" she asked, looking straight at him. "Well, *cousin* Peg, not bad, not a bad day at all, that's what I had."

Now Annie stared at him as well.

"What? Are you going to tell us or what?"

"I am not staying with Flo's cousin if that's what you mean," said Kieran.

"Kieran, tell them." Flo poked him in his side.

"Ouch, Flo, did you have to push that hard."

"I'll push you myself if you don't tell us what you did today." Annie was beginning to sound cross.

44

"Well, I went to Garston docks, to ask around, and somehow I slipped through the gate without being noticed." Now he had a big grin on his face. "When I got to a big barge just being unloaded of coal, this guy next to me said, 'Oi, you, don't laze about, get on with it.' So I did."

Now all three were hanging on his every word. "And then what?" Peg could not stand the suspense much longer.

"Well, I used my Irish charm, didn't I? Here." He put his hand into his pocket and in his outstretched hand was eleven shillings and two pence. A day's pay. "Wait, and here." He put his hand into his other pocket and got out a piece of paper. "I think this will be the address of my new lodgings, I will go there before work tomorrow. And now, who is going for some extra beer?"

Chapter 12

"I just started my job, how can I possibly go on strike?"

The friends were sitting at the 'The Gay Cavalier' pub close to Garston docks. They had already declared that this would be their 'local', although it was some distance from where Annie lived. It was the beginning of May, and the days were mild and the evenings light. Annie did not mind walking back to Allerton. All she had to do was go to Banks Road, short cut through the cinder path, the match works on the right, left on to Speke Road and not far on the right was the turn taking her to where she now lived. They were meeting at the pub on Fridays after work. As soon as the big whistle went at the bottle works, Annie's apron was off, and she hurried to see her friends.

"Don't be home too late, Annie!" shouted Peg after her.

But Annie was already through the gate. This would be the third time they had met there, and to Annie, it was already like home. She felt a bit guilty at that thought, only yesterday she had received a letter from her mam telling her how much she missed her and that her little brother, Paddy, was sure she would be back soon. Annie had cried and read the letter again and again. But that was yesterday. Now she would see her friends, and maybe Kieran would bring George along again. Annie felt herself blushing at that thought. They all had got on rather well, that was for sure.

"Do you have to go on strike?" Flo looked at Annie with concern.

"Peg said if the Trade Unions announce a General Strike, the bottle works will shut. Nobody will be able to go to work, there might not be any transport. Peg said even if Bob's metal factory was open, he could not get there. He has to take the tram each day. Peg said worst of all, there would be no money coming in and who knows how long the strike might last."

"Now, now, Annie, calm down, it might never happen." She felt George's hands on hers, and it had the opposite effect, instead of calming her as he suggested, her heart started to race and heat started rising to her face.

Oh, my God, she thought, he just noticed my red face.

"Yes, Annie, don't work yourself into a frenzy." Flo had noticed Annie's discomfort and came to her rescue. "What about you two, are you going on strike?" Flo now turned to Kieran.

"I will play it by ear. I don't want to upset the applecart." Both Flo and Annie now looked at him with a puzzled expression. When he did not enlighten them, Flo said, "What is that supposed to mean?"

"Well, Flo, since you are asking, this is how I see it. I can't just go on strike, or I might lose my job altogether, right? Also, I can't just turn up for work, or the other dockworkers will ostracise me."

"Ostracise you?"

"Alright, it is something I read at the cafe today. I think it means they'll be none too pleased. Therefore, Flo, I am going to do my usual and rely on my Irish charm."

"How?"

"If there is a strike, and I mean if, Annie will not work either, will you, Annie?"

"According to Peg, everything will be closed."

"So, I thought the four of us could meet up, like coincidentally, and go down to the docks. There we would find out what is going on. The pickets will not think we are breaking the strike because George and I are there with you lovely ladies."

"Kieran, you really have worked it out, I must hand it to you, however, I don't think the women in the wash house will go on strike. They would like to very much, believe you me, but for some families, the washing they do for others is the only money coming in to feed their children. That's where I will be."

"Maybe you can have a day off." When Kieran saw Flo's expression he quickly added, "But on the other hand, let's wait and see."

"Let's get some more beer," suggested George.

"Kieran, how is that new lodging of yours?"

"It's great," answered Flo. Seeing Annie raising her eyebrows in surprise, she realised what she had just said. "I mean, you said it is great, didn't you, Kieran?"

"So I did, yes, it is great. I pay my landlady twenty shilling a week and get food and lodgings. She lets all three rooms out and only uses the front parlour for herself. The kitchen is big enough for a table and chairs. I might even pay somebody to do my washing." He winked at Flo.

"In your dreams," she replied.

"Sorry, I will have to go soon – I promised Peg I would not be late. She still thinks I don't know the way home on my own."

"I'll walk you back," offered George, only now noticing he still had his hand on Annie's, and she had not pulled it away.

"Well, I'll be off. Same time next week, unless the strike has been called, in that case I will come over and find you either at the wash house or at your cousin's," Annie said to Flo. She gave Flo and Kieran a hug and left with George in tow.

Chapter 13

All talks between the miners' union and the government failed. A General Strike was announced by the Trade Unions. Starting date was one minute to midnight on 3 May 1926. The dispute was over miners' pay and conditions. Coal production had fallen in recent years, but the mining companies decided the revenue received for the output must remain the same as before. To achieve this, they insisted the pay of the miners was decreased and the hours of work increased. The union was fighting a losing battle and negotiations came to a standstill. Their argument was that in the last seven years miners' pay had been reduced from six pounds to three pounds eighteen shillings fell on deaf ears. The Trade Unions backed up the miners' union's position, and the strike was declared.

On the second day of the strike, when Annie was on her way to find Flo, she was confronted by groups of people marching through the street, holding banners that read, Not a penny off the pay, not a minute on the day. People were shouting the slogan whilst they walked towards the docks.

For a short distance, Annie was swept along with the crowd. As soon as she saw an opportunity, she stepped to the side unnoticed. Bob had told her that the strikers had a good point. Although most were not affected directly, it could be the other industries next. It was best to stick up for each other. He warned her not to voice her opinions to anybody she did not know. Annie found Flo at the wash house and told the woman in charge a lie, saying that Flo's cousin was not well and asking if she could please come home?

"Alright, lucky there is not much work today, you can go," she said to Flo. Before Flo had her pinny off, she added, "Don't make a habit of it."

They found Kieran and George waiting outside the pub and together, they walked towards the docks. They could not get to the gate, because it was blocked by the same group that Annie had come across earlier. By now, somebody had made a makeshift podium and a speaker was going to address everybody there. As soon as he started, the people started to push Annie and her friends forward. Before they could protest, they were at the front of the mob being pushed against the gate. "Kieran, Kieran, we need to get out of here, we are going to get squashed, do something," Flo managed to shout.

"Mate, open the gate, me and my friend here work over there, unloading the 'Scagerrag', our girls will suffocate, if we can't get them out."

The two men at the gate unlocked the chain and opened it about twelve inches. The four quickly squeezed through and helped to shut the gate behind them.

"That was close, are you alright, Annie?" George looked concerned. Annie was leaning against a railing, trying to catch her breath.

"I will be alright in a minute, but that was quite scary."

"Come on, we can't leave until everybody out front has left. We can find out what will be happening here, now the General Strike has been called. We can get some coffee over there." Kieran was pointing ahead, started to leave and the others followed.

George walked Annie home again. Peg spotted them through the front room window and signed for Annie to come in.

"I have to go George, see you soon."

"When?"

"Don't know."

"How about tomorrow?"

Peg was by now knocking on the window with some urgency.

"See you at the pub tomorrow then, Annie."

"George, Peg said we don't know how long the strike will last, could be weeks and meanwhile there is no money coming in. We don't even know whether there will be work to go back to. Let's wait for a little while. I'll see you soon." Annie felt awkward having given such a speech and kissed him on the cheek. "I will see you soon, promise," she said and ran inside. She was surprised to see her sister, Kate, sitting at the kitchen table with Peg.

"Kate, I did not know you would be here, has something happened?"

"No, not really."

"What do you mean?" Annie went over to the teapot poured herself a cuppa and sat at the kitchen table next to Peg, facing Kate. "Where is Bob?" Annie continued reaching for a piece of fruitcake, which she assumed Kate had brought with her.

"With William, in the front room, chatting."

"Why is William here as well, and why are they are chatting? Something is wrong, tell me."

"No, it is great news. Kate and William are moving two doors down, here in Stamfordham Drive. They have been on the Corporation waiting list for some time, and an exchange has come up."

"But that is fantastic. So why the long face?"

"William had himself enlisted to join the RAF," Kate said, wiping the tears, which were forming in her eyes, got her handkerchief out and blew hard into it.

"The RAF, but why? Did you know about it?"

"No, of course not, silly, why do you think I am so upset, especially now."

"What else don't I know?"

"Hello, Annie, did Kate tell you our good news?" William and Bob now entered the kitchen. William pulled a chair, offered it to Bob, who shook his head. William shrugged his shoulders and sat down.

"Yes, you are moving here, two doors down, and you are joining the RAF, but I am not sure whether the last one is good news."

"No, I don't mean that, we are having a baby."

Annie jumped out of her chair and went over to where her sister sat and put her arm round her shoulder. "Kate, that is wonderful news, congratulations. You will be living here and me being an aunt, I could not think of anything better."

Now Kate was really sobbing. William started to look uncomfortable.

"Look," he said, "I thought it was the best thing to do for a secure future for my family, especially with a baby coming along. Joseph said..." He was interrupted by a furious Kate.

"Joseph said? What has our life got to do with Joseph? Since when is he an expert on raising a family?"

"Now, now, Kate, Joseph has a point, more of our mates lost their jobs at the plant even before the strike. The unemployment is going up and up. Soon none of us will have work, and then what? What will you say when no money is coming in, and there is no food on the table for our baby, what will you say then?" William had left his seat and was now standing next to Bob.

William took a deep breath to calm himself down and continued, "Joseph was going to enlist today, he does have a little girl himself, you know. I only went with him to give him courage, and well, once there, I saw it made sense."

Kate had stopped crying and was looking at him. William never raised his voice before.

"We are to report to Leconfield next week." When he realised the name drew a blank, he added, "Beverley, North Humberside."

Still nobody spoke.

"Kate, I am going to provide for you and our child, whatever it takes." He had walked round to where Kate sat, she got off her chair, and he held her in his arms. He looked over her shoulder towards Annie and said, "Annie, why don't you put your name on the waiting list for a house, here, we could all live in the same street together."

Chapter 14

"Give me that!" Kieran grabbed the newspaper from the boy standing at the corner and handed him his tuppence.

"What does it say?" asked Flo and Annie at the same time.

Flying Scotsman derailed. Mob of striking miners attack train near Newcastle. Government is calling emergency meeting with Trade Unions. End of Strike action in sight.

"And not a day too soon, it has been nine days now, and we are really running out of money at my home. What about you?" Annie asked the others.

"Desperation here," said Kieran.

"No work at the wash house either. Who would have the spare money for somebody else to do their washing?" admitted Flo.

"Same situation as Kieran. Now with the strike action stopping, let's go and check at the docks to see when we can come back. Maybe we should also check at the bottle works. What do you think, Annie?"

"Yes, let's George and if the news is good, we will go for a drink. What do you think?"

Of course, everybody agreed to that suggestion.

Down at the docks, the gates were open, and the dockworker checking the men's working passes as they entered, spotted Kieran and George.

"Oi, you two. I have been looking for you, get back to work, unloading has started."

"Sorry, girls, but we have to go. See you Friday."

"See you. Let's check the bottle works, and then I'll go and see if there is any work for me at the wash house."

At the bottle works there was a notice attached to the door:

A decision has been made to open the plant for work tomorrow, Thursday 13 May 1926. All workers must report for normal duties.

"Peg will be pleased. I wonder whether Bob will go back to work as well. What about the trams?"

"Actually now you mention it, I have seen some activity down there earlier. I went over the square before we met, and a tram was just leaving. We can go that way to the wash house, if the trams are working, you can tell Bob when you get home."

When Annie got home full of all the good news, Peg already knew, and Bob had left for work. One of his mates called by the house and together they went off. Peg did not think he would be home until the morning.

"When do you think Kate will be moving in?" Annie asked Peg, helping to peel potatoes for the evening meal.

"I hope soon, now with William gone to the RAF training camp, she will be lonely in Birkenhead. If the Corporation office is open tomorrow, maybe we will have time to check after work, otherwise, on Friday. Why don't you put your name on the list whilst we are there?"

"George has put his name down some time ago, he told me."

"George? Oh, no, Annie, don't tell me."

"What? No. I am just saying he has put his name down, that's all."

Chapter 15

George now spent quite a few evenings at Annie's. The first time he went there on his own and uninvited it took all the courage he could muster. He searched high and low for a reason to go and knock on her door, worried what sort of reception he would get from Annie's sister, Peg, or her husband, Bob. But then, luck turned in his favour. Kieran and George had been unloading fruit. It was a consignment of bananas. Most of them still green, but part of them had gone yellow bordering on brown. He took both lots and stacked the wooden crates at the side of the dock on top of each other, as instructed in the morning.

"You have to take those off and put them against the wall over there, the yellow ones go directly to the market, the green ones go into the large hall over there on the right, see?" One of the workers pointed towards the building designated to hold the fruit.

"What's the difference?"

"The green ones can wait, but if we don't shift the yellow ones fast, they will go to waste. Look here, they will go soft, see, like these. Here, try one."

"Thanks, mate."

"Mmm, delicious," agreed George.

"Have another one, we can't load these on the lorry anyway."

"Can I take a few for my girlfriend?" He took some and showed them to the dock worker issuing all these instructions.

"Sure, but if you're caught, I know now't about it."

"I didn't know Annie was your girlfriend," said Kieran.

"Nor does she...Yet."

"And you think a few rotten bananas will swing it?"

"It's worth a try, I would say. It might swing that Peg over into my favour too."

Most of the time they were unloading coal, timber or steel, but on a few occasions, it would be something more useful to them, such as potatoes, root vegetables, or even tea, this was when a small vessel had been diverted from the Liverpool docks. Not that Peg objected when George brought along some coal, especially since it had become very cold all of a sudden. Kate's little girl was unwell with a high temperature, which was really worrying, her being only a few months old.

Peg was grateful that at least they now lived only two doors away, and it was easy for her or Annie to help out when Kate was tired, or not well herself. Kate had asked Annie to become godmother to her little girl. The christening would be in the spring. William was going to apply for leave from the RAF and as soon as it was granted, a date would be set.

But there was talk that William would be sent to the new headquarters being set up in Hong Kong and Kate had not seen him since he was transferred to Northolt. He had told her on his last leave that Joseph was in Shanghai already.

"Is George coming over tonight?" Peg asked Annie.

"I don't know, come to think about it, he's not been over all week. Why, what do we need?"

"That's not the only reason I asked after him, although it does help when he brings stuff along. We urgently need extra coal, it's freezing at Kate's, and little Shauna is not getting any better. Kate had to call the doctor again. He said there's a flu going round."

"I'm going to meet up with them tomorrow, and if Kieran has not seen George, maybe he knows what is wrong. I hope nothing has happened to him."

Friday, after the hooter went as usual, Annie could not wait to rush to their pub. She couldn't reveal to Peg how worried she was that they had not seen or heard from George. Maybe she had only imagined that he fancied her, and after she kissed him that last time he came over, she had scared him away.

Flo and Kieran were already in the pub waiting for her.

"Where's George?" was the first thing she asked.

"He's laid up with the flu, you know, the one that is going round. I saw him yesterday, and he looked awful. I told him to hurry up and get back to work, we're really short at the docks now, and loads of vessels are coming in. I don't think he even realised I was there."

"Kieran, you're not joking with me, are you? Is he really that bad?" Now Annie was even more worried than she had already been.

"His landlady is doing her best, but I think you should go and have a look at him yourself. To be honest, I am quite worried about the state of him."

"Sorry, but I have to go there now." Annie stood up, took her coat off the rack behind her and dropped her scarf and gloves. Her hands were shaking when she picked them back up. Outside the east wind was biting her face, she wrapped her scarf around tighter, and raised the collar of her coat for extra protection. The coat was far too thin for the icy blast. Almost like winter had come early this year. I must go and see whether I can find something warmer at a rummage sale tomorrow, she thought whilst she hurried along.

She had never been at George's digs before and was not sure what the landlady would make of it, him having a female visitor. After several loud knocks, the front door was opened by a small boy wearing his pyjamas under an oversized men's jacket with nothing on his feet.

"Who is it?" Annie heard a strained voice calling from inside the house.

"A woman."

"Is it the doctor?"

"Don't know."

"Can I come in?" Annie asked the young boy gently, and he stood aside.

In the hall, a sickly stench hit Annie, and she almost gagged, but quickly pulled herself together. "Where's your mam?" The boy pointed towards a door at the end of the hall.

Annie pushed against the door with her gloved hand. On the settee was a woman with a cloth on her forehead and a sick bowl next to her. Annie rushed inside with three large steps.

The woman looked at her deliriously. "Doctor, you came."

"I'm Annie, George's friend. Where is he?"

The woman lifted a weak arm pointing upstairs.

"I'll be back down in a minute." Annie managed to say before taking two steps at a time rushing upstairs. The first door she opened was empty, but a complete mess, every item of boys clothing strewn on the floor, an unmade mattress on the floor, drawers pulled out of the chest, and a few broken toys. The second door was locked, maybe another lodger's room. The last room's door was slightly ajar. Annie opened it with her foot, worried what she would find. George was on his back on a metal bed. A thin grey stained blanket covered a shivering body, other than that George did not move. "George, are you alright?" He did not respond. Annie was standing at his bedside, and could see his chest moving up and down, and heard his laboured breath. The bedding was soaked with sweat.

"Oh, my God, George!" She took her gloves off and felt his forehead. He was burning.

"George, please wake up." Annie shook him gently, and George opened his eyes.

"Annie, you are here," he whispered.

"George, you hang in there, you hear, I will get help."

Annie jumped down the stairs, past the little boy. "You wait here, I'll get help for your mam and George." Annie did not wait for a reply and ran all the way back to the pub, hoping Flo and Kieran were still there. She saw them just leaving and shouted, "Flo, Kieran, we need a doctor, quickly, hurry."

Within seconds, her friends were by her side. With few words, Annie told them the state of George and his landlady, but Kieran was already far ahead of them.

The Garston hospital was full to its capacity with flu patients, but the doctor Kieran managed to find insisted George and his landlady were admitted. Flo looked after the little boy and coaxed an address of his aunty from him. She got him dressed as best she could, took him by the hand and went off to find her, but first she took him to the little cafe at the bottom of St Mary's Road to get him a drink of milk and a sugary bun.

Chapter 16

"What do you mean you got engaged, Annie?"

"George and I, we got engaged. Engaged to be married. That sort of engaged."

Annie had worried all week how best to tell Peg her good news. It had happened so quickly. They all were out at their usual pub when George came storming through the door.

"Guess what?" He shouted as soon as the door opened. Not giving anybody one second to reply, he threw a piece of paper on to the table.

Kieran's hand was the first to reach it while George had gone to the bar.

"A round of drinks for my friends." They heard him say.

"Blimey, George, you got yourself one of those houses in Campania Street. How did you swing that?"

"Give me that." Now Flo wanted to see for herself.

"It says here, 'Dear Mister Marrion, we are happy to be able to offer you, number 4 Campania Street, which will become available at the end of 1927. Please give the name and address of your fiancée. A separate letter will be sent. If you decide to take up this offer, please contact the Corporation office for an appointment.' What fiancée?" She handed the letter to Annie with a puzzled look.

Annie was now holding it in her hand, trying to avoid looking at her friend. This was the first she had heard about it.

George had put all the glasses on to the small table. He stood next to Annie, who was by now staring at him. He reached into his trouser pockets and got out a small black box. He took Annie's left hand and opened the box. He got on to his knee and said, "Annie, I did this for us. Will you marry me?"

Annie seemed speechless, but George heard a softly whispered, "Yes."

"Did you hear that?" George shouted, and everybody in the pub now turned towards them.

"She said, yes!" George took the ring from the box and put it on to Annie's left hand. It was a little bit loose.

By now, Flo had jumped out of her seat and hugged her best friend. "Annie, that's wonderful, married and almost living next door. Oh, George, you are so romantic." Flo wiped the tears from her eyes. "Take note, Kieran, if you ever decide to make an honest woman of me, that is how to do it."

" I, I don't know what to say," stammered Annie.

"You already said yes. You heard her, didn't you?" shouted George to everybody around him. To Annie's embarrassment, people were now applauding and coming over to congratulate her.

"Let's have a look at your ring." Flo was recovering from her shock of what had just happened. "It looks expensive, George, how did you manage that?"

George shrugged his shoulders. "Nothing is too expensive for my Annie," he said, taking Annie's ringed hand and gazing into her eyes.

"No, seriously, George, how did you afford it?"

"With overtime at the docks." Now Kieran was the one to look at him. "I managed to put a deposit down," George now confessed. "Annie, don't worry, I have it all worked out."

"You have to take it back." Annie took the ring off her finger and handed it back to George.

"No, Annie, please," pleaded George.

"George, it's too big, they have to make it smaller. Also,

this way I will not arrive home tonight with a ring on my finger. I think I'll have to tell Peg about it a little bit later," a now worried Annie said.

"Let's celebrate," was Kieran's solution to most problems.

"Please, Annie, tell me you're joking," Peg still could not believe what Annie had just said.

"Peg, it's true, I am getting married. I'll be eighteen soon."

"Please don't misunderstand, I do like George, sort of."

"Sort of?"

"Annie, sorry to say, he's an unskilled labourer. What future would you have? I want something wonderful for you."

"I have something wonderful, thank you. I love George, and there is nothing you can say to make me change my mind." Annie had worried that her announcement would end up with her fighting with her sister.

"Annie, besides everything else he is English and a Protestant!"

Chapter 17

Annie started the letter to her parents. She looked at it, crumpled it up and put it in the bin. No, those words would not do. She was sitting at the kitchen table. Peg had gone to church this morning, and Bob was still sleeping. Bob had been really happy for her when Peg had told him the news. He wanted to make plans with her there and then. Only Peg's look curbed his enthusiasm. "I'll go to bed then," he had said, but at the bedroom door he turned round and winked at Annie. She breathed a sigh of relief, at least she had one ally.

In the end, Annie's letter turned into almost a short story. She told them about her life in Liverpool, her friends and her work and all the places she had already seen. This was something she should have done a long time ago. Annie felt guilty that her usual letters where rather short. She told them how she had met George, that she had fallen in love, about the possibility of somewhere for them to live. That they were going to get married when she turned eighteen. She hoped she would have their blessing, and she confessed that George was English and a Protestant. That was the reason they would get married at the Garston registry office and not in a church. Sister Theresa at her old school will have a fit, when she finds out, Annie thought. She told her parents that they were planning only a small wedding party in a separate room at their local pub, and that she hoped they would come.

She then enclosed a ten bob note for Paddy. Annie tried to put some pennies or a shilling in her bedside drawer each week. When she had saved enough to change it into a ten bob note, she would send it to him in one of her letters home. She knew her mam would always give it to him. Paddy had told her on the one occasion he wrote back, that he is hiding it and saving it for when he comes to live in Liverpool, just like her.

Her friends had decided that Annie and George's engagement needed to be celebrated. But Annie was already adding up all the costs of their future life together and doubts whether they could afford to get married, started to creep in.

"For goodness sake, Annie, we can't just let an occasion like that pass by without a do."

Flo could be very insistent. The four of them settled to go to the cinema in Woolton village. The Woolton picture house was showing a new film, *Carry On!* starring Moore Marriott, Trilby Clark and Alf Goddard. They could go there by tram and have a beer in the pub opposite after the show.

But Annie's biggest worry was not how they would be able to afford to live by themselves, or where they would get furniture from, or even that they had no savings put by for a new household. Annie's immediate worry was, 'I have nothing to wear'. They had already set a date, 12 January 1928. This date was largely due to the fact that the house in Campania Street was empty as from Saturday the 14th. The registrar at the town hall told them the only day available for a wedding would be the Friday, but there was no way Annie was going to get married on a Friday the 13th. She pleaded with the registrar, who shook his head. No, there was no space available. Only Annie's tears finally persuaded him, and he fitted them in at a quarter to twelve on the Thursday.

"Flo, what am I going to wear?"

"You are in luck, Annie, my cousin kept her wedding

dress and one of the women at the wash house has a sewing machine. I have already talked to her. She has agreed to alter it for you. But we must go ahead with it straight away. She has quite a bit of work before Christmas."

"How much will it cost?"

"It is my wedding gift for you, and my cousin does not want it back either. She says she's throwing the miserable bugger out soon anyway."

"This will not bring me bad luck will it?"

Flo had gotten used to Annie's superstitious mind and simply ignored it. "The woman could alter my bridesmaid dress at the same time. I am your bridesmaid, am I not?"

Chapter 18

George introduced Annie to his family. Although his dad, together with George's brothers, Albert and Norris, plus his sister, Beattie, lived very close to the docks, Annie had never met them before. George took Annie to his family home in Vulcan Street just before Christmas. He knocked on the back door, even though he still had a house key. Young Norris opened the door.

"Did you know me mam died nearly three years ago?" Is how he greeted her.

"Yes, Annie knows that, Norris," replied George and pulled Annie in front of him and pushed her along the hall towards the front room.

"She had something wrong with her lungs," Norris continued, walking behind George. "They said that's what killed her. But me dad says she died of a broken heart because our George left home."

"What are you trying to do, Norris?" asked George without turning round.

"Nothing, I am just telling Annie, about me mam." George opened the door to the front room. "Dad, I brought Annie along, she is here to meet you."

His dad was sitting with his back to them, in an armchair, in front of a small open fire. All Annie could see was the top of his head, which was starting to go bald.

"Close the door son, you are letting the heat out."

"Who is Annie, son?" he then asked.

"I told you we are getting married."

"When?"

"Dad, can you please stand up and say hello to my fiancée, Annie."

George's father slowly rose from his chair. He was wearing his undershirt, which was stained, and the braces of his trouser were down, touching the linoleum on the floor as he stood up. He came over to where Annie stood. She had not moved one inch since she entered the room.

He stretched out his hand and said, "Miss Annie, welcome to my house. Excuse the state of me. I have not been home long. Been working at the docks. I was unloading coal all day and must have fallen asleep in front of the fire." Annie shook his hand.

"We should have told you we were coming today," said Annie.

"But we..." George was starting to say, then he saw Annie's warning look, the look she was so good at, and stopped.

"Yes, we should have, Dad. Sorry. Norris, get our dad a shirt." He turned round to his little brother who was still inside the doorway, gawping at the scene in front of him.

George looked at his young brother and indicated with his head to go upstairs and fetch what he had just asked for.

"Mister Marrion, shall I make us a cup of tea? My sister Peg has baked this fruitcake."

"Call me John, no need to be this formal, Miss."

"Please call me Annie."

Norris had re-entered the room and gave his father a crumpled but clean shirt.

"Norris, why don't you and me put the kettle on. We can cut my sister's cake. "Dad, look at the state of you..." she heard George's voice as she closed the front room door behind her. The kitchen was small, but spotless and tidy. At the back wall an open fireplace. A rack with washing in front of it, although the fire was not lit. On one side next to the sink, a gas stove on tall legs. On the shelf below, scrubbed saucepans. The floor looked recently swept. A wooden table on the other side with three assorted chairs. Clean dishes neatly stacked at the side of the sink. Norris took one chair, pulled it over to a wall cupboard and climbed on. He handed Annie three chipped, but clean, mugs.

"Annie, at your house, do you have Christmas decorations?"

"Yes, Norris. Bob got us a Christmas tree, and last year we made our own tree ornaments, which we kept. The tree is up already."

"We had a tree, when me mam was still alive."

Annie did not want to show young Norris how upset she was for him, and tried to play the conversation down. "What about your sister, Beattie, does she not decorate the house with you."

"She is always out, with that fella of hers, we hardly ever see her."

"Who does the cooking then?"

"Nobody."

"Nobody?"

"Because I have no mam, I get a free meal at school. Me dad finds something at work, or at the pub, which he goes to."

"What about your sister Beattie and your brother Albert?"

"Don't know, they don't eat here. Beattie is a real 'meany', even if she brings biscuits home from work, she would eat them in front of me and not give me any."

Annie had heard enough. "Norris, would you like us to have Christmas here with you and your dad this year?" The lad dropped a mug on to the kitchen floor.

"Do you really mean it? You would come to my house? But we have nothing for a Christmas dinner."

"Let's take the tea to George and your dad, we can talk about it together. What do you think?"

Chapter 19

Annie looked lovely on her wedding day. To her delight, the dress, which Flo's cousin had given her, was beautiful. A dress like this one belongs in a movie, she thought as she touched the delicate fabric. She placed it to her face for the umpteenth time to feel the soft lace. What would George think when he saw her in it?

"Are you sure your cousin does not want it back?"

"Annie, how often do I have to tell you, no. What are you going to do with it afterwards anyway?"

"I'll keep it."

"What for?"

"I'll save it for my own daughter, so she can feel as beautiful as I do right now."

"Annie, is there something you have forgotten to tell me?" Flo was looking suspiciously at Annie's waistline.

"No, I kept myself for my wedding night, like a good Catholic Irish girl."

"You didn't?"

"What do you think?"

"You scare me sometimes, Annie, that's what I think." They both burst out laughing.

"Let's close your dress at the back, if it is tighter than when we tried it on after the alteration, I'll soon find out what you have been up to, Annie McGlynn."

"A soon to be married Annie, if you please."

Flo helped Annie to straighten out her dress. The white lace came all the way to the floor, covering the plain white satin underneath. The dress had a slight waistline. Not too tight, as Annie pointed out immediately. Delicate lace short sleeves. Annie's favourite was her lace veil. It sat like a lace cap on her dark hair. Flo had helped Annie earlier in the morning to put her hair up and then used hairpins to secure the veil. The veil went down to her waist and flowed over her shoulders. Annie knew it was freezing outside, but she did not care.

If Annie looked pretty and petite, Flo, in her dress, looked majestic. Her colourful printed chiffon dress reached to halfway up her calf. It was sleeveless, and a long row of plain purple beads hanging from Flo's neck matched some of the flowers on the dress perfectly. However, it was the turban style hat that made the real statement. After Annie had stood back and been admired by her best friend, Annie said again, "Flo, you look wonderful, almost oriental. You still have not told me where you got your dress from."

"Alright, I borrowed it for the day."

"What? Where from?"

"Let's just say, I hope the woman who brought it into the wash house, to see whether I could remove the stain at the front, does not need it today."

"Flo!"

"Why? I removed the stain, just as she asked."

Annie had stayed overnight with Flo in Campania Street. From here it was not too far to walk to the registry office. She knew that her dad would collect her and together they would walk the short distance. But she did not expect to see her mother and Paddy, her younger brother, standing next to him at the front door. Paddy was holding a small bunch of flowers.

Annie immediately burst into tears when she saw her family. They had all arrived from Ireland and only just made it in time.

Annie had never felt this happy before. She walked with

her dad, down the long room to where George was waiting for her in front of the registrar. George's eyes sparkled with pride when he saw his wife to be. He greeted Annie's mam and dad and Annie took her place next to him.

Chapter 20

The first few nights of Annie and George's life together were spent in the spare bedroom at Peg's, in Stamfordham Drive.

The newlyweds went furniture hunting. Most of what they ended up with was either donated by people they knew or came from Frank Kett, the pawnbroker down at the docks. For a bed, a small kitchen table, two chairs, a small worn-out sofa and an armchair, they had to go to the auction room. They got it all for eleven shillings. Kieran asked a mate at work whether they could use the small lorry, which was used to deliver sacks of coal, and if he would drive it for them and give them a hand. For another four shillings, he did. It took Annie and Flo three evenings, after work, to get rid of the coal dust from the furniture and from inside the house. They got a mattress, bedding and bedclothes from the pawnbroker together with some saucepans for a total of three shillings. Not a bad deal, they thought at the time, until they found out the mattress and pillows were flea ridden. By the time they noticed, it was already too late. Annie and George had red bite marks all over their bodies.

Annie had learned from her mother that a good remedy would be to place an aluminium bowl under the bed filled with soapy water. The fleas would drop down and stay on the surface of the water. Annie did this for several days until no more fleas appeared. Then she sprinkled some yeast on top of the mattress and pillow. They put it in the back yard in the winter sunshine. One of her new neighbours had a willow cane. George beat the mattress when he came home from work. Also, George had managed to scrounge a piece of lemon. Annie squeezed every last drop of it into some warm water. With a cloth, she rubbed it over the mattress and pillows. Home, at last. Annie was in her very own home. They had worked out how they would manage with the wages they earned between them. It was fortunate that George had work on most days, although some of his mates had been laid off, or only had enough work for three days a week.

But George was a mate of Kieran, and Kieran had the gift of the gab. He never missed an opportunity and made friends, especially with the dock foreman. This gave him inside information. He knew in advance which ships would dock the following week and how many men were needed. In return for this information, Kieran managed to find the odd bottle of Irish whiskey and handed it over when nobody was around. Once George asked him where he got it from.

"I am Irish, George, little green leprechauns whisper to me at night," was all he would say.

Life for Annie and George was good. George's hard work meant he brought home on average, a weekly wage of three pounds, fifteen shillings and five pence. With Annie's money, they could afford to pay for the rent, kept coins in a tin to feed the gas meter and still have some left over to buy a sack of coal for the fireplace in the kitchen and the front room, plus whatever was needed each week to make the agreed repayments of loans to the Co-op. This was for items they had purchased from the big store in town. Annie and George even managed to meet up with their friends most Friday afternoons for a pint at their local pub.

"Shall we go into Liverpool on Sunday? There is a summer fete near Pier Head," Flo suggested. When Annie did not immediately reply, Flo continued, "Come on, what is the matter with you? We have not been out all summer."

Kieran and George walked over from the bar with their drinks. "What was that you said, Flo?"

"How about all of us going to Pier Head on Sunday."

"Sounds good to me." Kieran looked at Annie and then at George. "What about it?"

"Yes, let's." Annie was sipping on her small glass of Guinness.

"I don't know, Kieran."

"Why not, George? What's the problem?"

"No, problem really, but there is a rumour going round in the neighbourhood that my Annie has to work because I don't bring in enough wages to look after my wife."

"What? George, don't listen to them. Annie, you like your work don't you?"

"Of course I do."

"That is settled then, we are going on Sunday, and that's that." Flo put her glass down firmly on to the small table, which almost toppled over. The glass of Guinness Annie held in her hand shook, and the drink spilled on to her dress. Annie, shocked by the unexpected shower, jumped up.

"Sorry, Annie." Flo had joined her and tried to brush the liquid on to the floor. At Annie's stomach, Flo's hand came to a sudden stop.

"Annie?"

"Annie what?" asked George.

Flo and Annie just looked at each other.

"Kieran, go to the bar and get Annie a new drink. I'll come with you."

"What is the matter with those two today?" whispered Kieran when they stood at the bar ordering a half of Guinness.

"Kieran, I think Annie has to tell George something."

"What?"

"Kieran, in a crisis you can be a real fast thinker, but sometimes you can be really thick."

Chapter 21

"Stay, don't leave me. Please!" Annie pleaded with Flo. "I'm so scared."

Flo bent down and put the flannel back into the bowl of cold water on the floor next to the bed. She wrung it out and wiped the sweat off Annie's forehead. George was pacing up and down, looking at the gold pocket watch his father had given him as a wedding present. The watch had belonged to his grandfather. Every time he showed it to Kieran, he would say, "My family heirloom."

"George, for Christ's sake! Stop looking at your watch. Go downstairs and boil more hot water. The midwife should be here in a minute."

"What if she's late? What if Kieran couldn't find her? What if she can't use her bike in the snowstorm? What if...?"

Annie grabbed Flo by the hand. "Yes, Flo, what then?" Annie's dark brown eyes pleaded with Flo.

"See what you've done, you've scared Annie."

Annie sat up in bed, buckled forward and screamed.

"Did you time that George, did you check how long ago the last contraction was?"

"You told me not to look at my watch."

"Annie, your husband is useless, tell him to go and wait downstairs and boil more water."

Flo had stayed in Annie and George's spare room for the last two weeks. She was worried about her friend. The doctor had told Annie to stop working a couple of months earlier. On one of the check-ups, he found Annie had a heart murmur, but he could not be sure whether it was related to her pregnancy. Flo had promised Annie not to tell George about it, and Annie only left her job two weeks before her due date.

Annie had asked Flo on her last day of work to meet her outside the gate. Flo presumed Annie found it difficult to walk home on her own, especially since this year there seemed to be no end to the harsh winter. It was near the end of February already. When Flo got to the bottle works, Annie was standing outside in the cold. Flo cursed herself for being late. Annie looked freezing. Her coat was open at the front. It was not big enough to cover her swollen stomach. Snow was covering Annie's scarf. "Sorry, Annie, that old witch at the wash house wouldn't let me go." Now Flo noticed a man standing behind her.

"Mister Harris, this is my friend, Flo, I told you about."

"You better not be late Monday morning, Flo. We start at 7am, and you'd better be as good as Annie here has led me to believe."

Flo stared at him open mouthed. "I, I will not be late and thank you," stammered Flo.

When the two friends were alone, Flo hugged her best friend. "Annie, how did you do that?"

"You didn't think I'd let my job go to a total stranger, did you?" Annie had laughed for the first time in weeks.

"Arrrrrrrrgh," Annie screamed again. Flo did not let on how worried she was herself. She never imagined it would be up to her to deliver Annie's baby alone. She wished Peg, Annie's sister, were here, but Peg had had a little boy just before Christmas. Flo was relieved when she heard voices downstairs.

"Annie, the midwife is here."

George burst through the door. "Kieran found the midwife."

"Now, George, why don't you just leave everything up to us? Fetch more towels." The robust looking midwife, with the most re-assuring smile, walked into the bedroom. She put her hand into the bucket of water standing on the side of the room. "This is too cold. Make yourself useful, if you don't mind, and bring some warm water."

Flo got up to leave. "Do you mind staying? Your friend needs you," the midwife said to Flo, whilst washing her hands in the bowl of water on top of a chest.

"Now let's have a look at you, Annie." She lifted the bedclothes and started to feel Annie's stomach. Then she got out her stethoscope and listened to the baby's heartbeat. "You have a strong little one in there. I just have to check your dilation."

Annie screamed again.

"You are doing really well, not long now. When I tell you to push, you push, alright Annie?" Annie managed a faint nod and sunk back on to her pillow. Her eyes never left Flo. Flo was wiping Annie's forehead again. Annie grabbed Flo's hand. "Flo, I can't do this," she cried.

"Yes, you can, Annie, with the next contraction I want you to push," replied the midwife.

"Arrrrrrrrrgh, arrrrrrgh."

"That's good, and again, push."

"Arrrrrrrgh, arrrrrrrrrgh, arrrrrrrrrrrgh."

"Good, I can see the head. Now with the next contraction you have to go all the way, don't stop pushing."

"Arrrrrrrrrrrrrrgh."

"Now push."

"You've done it Annie, it's a girl. You have a lovely little girl."

Chapter 22

"No, George! How could we afford to move into the tenements in Speke Road? It's two extra shillings a week."

"I know, Annie, but look at it from my point of view. Here we have to burn a lot of coal to keep us from freezing to death in the winter. Look at the gap in the windows. All the heat goes out and all the cold comes in. There we have neighbours below and on top of us. If we have nothing to burn in the stove, it would not be that critical."

"The fortune teller told me good things are coming to our house," Annie replied.

"Don't tell me you went to the dreadful woman again, only to part with the last of our money? Good things are coming to this house? How stupid does she think we are? You are seven months pregnant, of course goods things are coming to our house."

George had raised his voice, then started to pace up and down holding his head.

"George, what's wrong?"

"It's these headaches again, sometimes they get so bad I want to scream. Anyway, Annie, I spoke to Kieran, and it is all settled."

"What is settled?"

"Well you know Kieran, always full of bright ideas. Right?"

"Right."

"I told him that we need a bigger place with the second baby due soon. So he told me to go to the Corporation and apply for one of those flats in Speke Road Gardens. He heard somebody was moving out. So Kieran and I went to the office last week and sure enough they have one on the third floor, number 3b. Whilst there, Kieran told them he should be due to get our house here for Flo and himself."

"For Flo and himself? But you have to be married to get a place, and I did not even know they were thinking about it."

Grace, who had been asleep on a cushion in front of them on the piece of carpet in their front room, heard them talking and woke up. Grace was now one-and-a-half years old. She had started to walk on her own two months before and already had said her first words. George insisted her first word was 'dada'.

Little Grace was, to Annie's delight, a really good baby. Always a happy face. She now sat up, looked at her parents and sure enough, walked over to her father, who was still rubbing his temples to make his headache disappear.

"There you are Grace, you tell your mum we want to move into a really nice place, so you can play with all the other little girls and boys."

"Hold on, George, I'll just get her a bottle, and don't you disappear before you tell me about Kieran and Flo."

Annie left her armchair and supported her back with both hands. She could not wait for this pregnancy to be over. The doctor had advised her against having another child so soon after Grace was born. He wanted to run some tests on her heart first, but Annie never went back for the test and only saw the doctor again when he spotted her at the midwife's down at the docks.

"Anyway, where was I?" said George when Annie had given her little girl the bottle, which she happily took and sat back on the floor.

"Ah, yes, as I said, Kieran told them, they promised him the first house, which came free in Campania Street. Of course, they could not find any records of it and almost refused. Kieran, however, seemed upset, almost sobbing, said they had arranged the wedding on their promise. His mum and dad were arriving from Ireland, what would he tell them now?"

Annie was stunned and was just going to speak when George continued. "That was it. I signed for the apartment and Kieran has our house."

"I am surprised Flo did not tell me that they are getting married."

"Don't be, typically Kieran, she knows nothing about his plans."

Chapter 23

Annie's whole family were there when Annie and George got to their new flat in the tenements at Speke Road Gardens in October 1930. Flo was moving into Campania Street on the same day.

"I am not going to leave the house empty for even one night," she had declared to Annie.

"Somebody else might just move in. You know how long the list is for a fine house like yours." Flo had hugged her friend again when they loaded the last of Annie and George's possessions on to the handcart for the fifth load that day.

"Worth getting married for, is it?" Annie teased her friend. She had loved her little house, but she was happy that it was Flo who was moving into it.

"I'll come and see you tonight and help you unpack, I promise." She put her arms around Annie again and waved after her until Annie, with Grace by the hand, had moved round the corner.

There was a big welcoming party when Annie and George arrived with the last cart. Annie was huffing and puffing by the time she climbed three sets of stairs. She had noticed that she was out of breath a lot lately. Must be this pregnancy, she thought. Yes, the sooner the baby arrives the better.

Most of her new neighbours were outside gawking at the new arrivals. Some of them stepped forward and introduced themselves and some of them helped with the unloading. Older boys were eager to carry the few belongings upstairs and run quickly up and down the staircase, almost knocking her over on the way up. I hope George has a few pennies for them, she thought when she finally touched her new front door.

The door was slightly ajar, and she heard lots of voices from the inside. Annie had never been to her apartment before. She only had a description from George and Kieran who had a mate in one of the blocks. From what they told her, she tried to imagine what it would be like living there. She did this late at night in bed when she failed to fall asleep worrying about their future.

George seemed oblivious to their money problems. He thought that if he handed over nearly two pounds ten shillings a week, that should take care of everything. One night, she had caught him writing something into a little black book and hiding it in the bedside table. When he was out at the docks the next day, she tried to find it, but it was no longer there.

She pushed her front door fully open and took a first look at her new home. In front of her was a hallway and you could turn left or right. The noises from inside seemed to come from the left, so Annie decided that's where she should go. She entered the first room. The room was full of people all standing with their backs to her, in a circle, talking and laughing. This is my new front room. Somebody had put some music on. She heard 'Goodnight Sweetheart' from a wireless and then heard her two sisters, Peg and Kate, joining in. The smell of beer made her nauseous, and she was just going to turn around when William, Kate's husband, spotted her. He must have come home on leave, she thought the same moment as George shouted, "We are here."

"Annie!" William was the first one to hug her. "Annie, let me introduce you to my mate, Joseph." A dark-haired man stepped from behind William. His Air Force uniform seemed to swamp him. Smoke from his cigarette was drifting upwards and joined with the hazy mist from the other smokers. Through the cloud, she could make out his narrow face with sunken cheeks and haunting eyes. Annie started coughing. He came over and said, "I hope you do not mind me coming along. Joseph, Joseph McGreavy is my name."

Annie had no time to reply now, her sisters came over. Kate took Grace, who until then had held on to Annie's hand very tightly, "Look, Grace, your cousins are over there, they have been waiting for you all morning." But Grace started crying and Annie lifted her up.

"I think it is all too much for her, it is great to see you, but maybe we should just have some time to settle in tonight. I am really tired," Annie managed to say.

"You are right, everybody out," shouted Peg and kissed Annie on her cheek. "I'll come over during the week and help you."

Chapter 24

"I don't know how I can thank you, Flo, I will pay you back, honest."

"Annie, look at me. Now promise me you'll never ever, ever to go to a money lender again. They are sharks. Especially the woman you went to. Tell me again what happened."

"You remember when George was not well a few weeks ago? I thought he had a fever. He was hallucinating, that's how bad it was. Said people were after him. I took his gold watch to be pawned to pay the doctor. When he came, he prescribed some medicine. I needed money to pay for it, Flo. I had heard about the money lender from a neighbour. I asked her whether she knew where she was. She said not to worry, she would call on me when the money lender is down our street. She usually comes every two days. Meanwhile the neighbour gave me the money to go to the chemist but I had to promise to give it back to her the same week. Her husband would notice that some money was missing," she said. Annie took a deep breath and continued.

"When the money lender arrived downstairs in the centre of all the tenements, I first thought she was just a regular woman selling fish from the market. I only wanted to borrow four shillings, but on top of it, she also made me buy her stinking rotten fish for another two shillings. Now I owed her six plus interest. But it was for George's medicine, so what could I do?"

Annie saw Flo looking in despair at her. "What happened then?"

"Well, I could not pay her back at the end of the week. She came to our front door with some big men and threatened me. George was home, of course." Now Annie was sobbing.

"It's alright, Annie, you've paid her back now. But next time you come straight to me, what are friends for?"

"But you gave me your savings. I will pay you back, each week a little bit. I am so ashamed, Flo." Annie felt a stabbing pain at her heart. She put her hands where her pain was and breathed in slowly.

"Annie, are you alright? You look so pale."

"Don't worry, it must have been from the money lender's rotten fish." Now they both looked at each other and and Annie managed a weak smile.

"I hope George will have a full week's work again. I really could do with finding a job myself."

"What, with three little children?"

"Grace could get a place in a kindergarten. Freda on the first floor is sending her boy there, and she had heard they have more places. But to get her in, I need a valid reason for sending her there." Grace heard her name and stopped playing on the kitchen floor with Jeffrey. "Mam, I want to go to the kindergarten and play with the other children."

"Yes, I know, you will my dear, you will. Now be a good girl and check on your little sister."

"I think the Co-op down the road in Garston need a cleaner. It would be very early in the morning and late in the evening. What do you think?"

"That would be difficult because George works all hours, but a cleaning job in the afternoon at some company office would be great. I could leave Grace at a neighbour after kindergarten and take Jeffrey and Dorothy with me."

"I will keep a look out for you, as well. I should have a lot of time on my hands now what with Kieran going to sea."

"That must have been a big decision for him. Leaving you behind and spending week after week at sea."

"Yes, but the pay is regular. The payment of two thirds of his wages will come directly to me. That is twenty-five shillings each week. The rest is paid at each end of their trips. Plus, when he is in-between voyages, the men are getting unemployment benefits."

"But you'll hardly see him."

Flo looked at Annie and George's three children and sighed.

"Yes, I know, Annie."

Chapter 25

12 May 1937

"Long live the king," shouted George, raising his glass of beer in salute. "To King George the VI, I could not have picked a better name for a king myself," he laughed.

Although it was a Wednesday, George did not go to work at the docks. They had just finished unloading a consignment of coal during the night. It was always one of the most backbreaking jobs there was. Some of the workmen were below deck shovelling the coal into hessian sacks. Others carried the sacks on their shoulders, up the steps and dropped them on the deck above. A third dockworker heaved it back on to his back and carried it down the plank and dropped it in front of a waiting lorry. Others then loaded the sacks on to the lorry. George had heard that down at the Liverpool docks they had new cranes fitted to lift the filled sacks from the bottom of the boat on a platform all the way on to the dockside. A fine thing that would be, he had thought when he almost buckled under the weight of a full sack on a ladder. On the other hand, at least most of his mates here in Garston docks had work. If there would be some sort of investment into those fancy cranes, who knows how many workers were needed. Yes, he decided it was better the way the coal was unloaded here, especially now. He counted himself lucky. So far he had never been laid off since the day he started, if you don't count the days of the General Strike or when he was ill, that is. Only the other week, he had been really unwell at work and went home early, but he had not told Annie anything about it. George had pretended it was his allocated free time and went back to work sooner than he should. Annie never knew he did not have a full pay packet that week. Tomorrow, another load, this time big bars of steel, was coming in. At least three hard days slogging in a row, but the foreman had put him inside the vessel to oversee the correct attachment, making sure the load did not slip off. This was the job everybody was after, it was less backbreaking. He often wondered why he was favoured or why he was always the first one to be picked for work when the schedule was announced. Did Kieran have anything to do with it? He had seen him slipping something into the foreman's pocket when he was on his latest home leave. He noticed Kieran looking at the foreman's face but nodding in the direction to where George was standing. He had thought George was not looking.

Annie came into the front room, from the kitchen, with a couple of bottles of beer for them all to share. Flo, Peg and Kate refilled their glasses. The children were sitting on the floor, wearing the crowns they had made from cardboard earlier in the week. There was no school today. Grace, Jeffrey, Dorothy and their cousins, were busy trying to find all the right pieces for a jigsaw puzzle Flo had found in a rummage sale. She had waited until today to give it to them.

"Come on, Annie, you sit down. George, you should not let Annie do all the running around and carrying. The doctor said she should have a lot of rest during her pregnancy."

Peg was getting cross with George.

"Do you think this new king of ours will manage to avoid a war with Germany?" George directed his question towards Bob who was half listening to the BBC broadcast of the coronation of King George VI and Queen Elizabeth.

"What war? There will be no war. Will there, Bob?" Annie perked up at the mention of war.

"William thinks there will be," replied Kate instead. "He said I should prepare myself in case we are at war with Germany."

"But how do we prepare for a war?"

"He did not say."

George now realised what he had done. All the women in the room looked scared and today was supposed to be a celebration.

"Annie, don't worry, that mad bloke Hitler is all hot air, he will never dare to declare war on us, you mark my words."

Chapter 26

30 September 1938

"Read all about it! Read all about it! Peace for our time. Chamberlain negotiates peace with Germany!"

George grabbed the newspaper from the paperboy standing outside the docks.

"Oi, you have to pay for that, mister."

George turned round and handed him tuppence. He had been right, there would be no war. His Annie would be pleased when he came home with such good news. She had been so down lately. Now he could cheer her up, he read the paper whilst he hurried along.

He still could not believe it when she had said 'yes' all those years ago. Things had not gone smoothly since then. He was the first to admit that. I better check how much money I have left in my box, he thought. Maybe I can take her away for a few days. Yes, that's what I will do. Take her away and give her a good time. Blackpool, yes, we are going to Blackpool. Without the kids, maybe Peg can look after them, or maybe Flo. He was sure Flo would agree immediately. He had seen the way she looked at Annie sometimes, when Annie seemed out of breath. But would Annie leave baby Derek behind? He doubted it. Derek already managed to pull himself up and was happy to sometimes feed himself when he sat in the high chair. Derek loved his food. Surely Flo could manage to cook some vegetables, mix it with boiled potatoes and mash it all up. That's what Annie said Derek liked best. Yes, I will ask her to look after Derek. The others could walk to Peg's house at the end of the school days, it was not that far. I'll check with the foreman tomorrow; maybe he knows some place in Blackpool, they could just turn up and rent a room for a few days. Can't be busy in Blackpool right now. The new school year had started a few weeks back, and the autumn break would not be for another three weeks. Yes, a good time to go.

He almost whistled when he took the steps to their apartment two at a time, put the key into the lock and shouted, "Annie, guess what." He could hear the wireless and Chamberlain's voice boomed out:

My good friends, for a second time in our history, a British prime minister has returned from Germany bringing peace with honour. I believe it is 'peace for our time'. Go home and get a nice quiet sleep.

"Did you hear that Annie, no war, just peace. What did I tell you? Annie?"

He reached the kitchen and first saw Derek in his highchair, happily spooning some goo from a small dish in front of him. Some of it had spilled on to the kitchen floor, and Derek looked down to see where it had gone. George followed to where Derek was looking.

"Annie!" With two steps, he was by her side. He lifted her head off the floor, and Annie opened her eyes.

"Annie, what happened?" He helped her to stand up.

"Don't fuss, George, I must have slipped."

Chapter 27

"Lucky I didn't agree to go away to Blackpool, Peg. We could have never afforded it, despite what George said and now it's too late anyway, with all this hanging over our heads."

"Are you considering sending your children then? That would be the right decision to make Annie."

Annie just looked at her

"Just think about it, that's all I am asking you. Just think about it."

"Peg, be reasonable, how can you ask me to think about it? For one thing, we don't have the money, and secondly, little children have to be accompanied by their mothers."

"You could send Grace, Jeffrey and Dorothy with their teachers, the same way we are sending our two."

"And then what, I take one-year-old Derek in his pram, abandon George and go off to who knows where? And in case you have forgotten, I am about to have another child in a few weeks."

"Yes, so you are." Peg sighed and gave in.

"But they are also moving young mothers, especially pregnant women." Peg tried once more.

"Where are you going to send the two of yours to?" Annie decided there was no point arguing with Peg, she knew how Peg was worried about her.

"The teacher said the Liverpool Corporation is arranging for places in Cheshire and north Wales."

"You don't even know where your children are going?"

"No, we just have to pack some small cases, one for each child in case they get separated. Their name, school number and home details go on a bit of cardboard around their necks. We have already been issued with the tags. We are also putting their names and our address on the suitcase, plus a piece of paper inside it and a piece of paper with our contact details into their coat pockets."

"Peg, don't do it, what if they get lost, or God forbid, one or both of them end up going on one of those big boats taking them all the way to Canada, even Australia, I have heard somebody say so."

"Don't be silly, Cheshire or Wales, that's where my lot end up, you'll see."

"What has Kate decided to do with her children?"

"She is as stubborn as you, she wants to keep them at home with her, but I think when William is back on home leave next week, she will have no choice but do as he says."

Annie stopped pouring the tea into her best china cup, the one reserved for visitors.

"What do you mean, has no choice?"

"Don't get me wrong, I just think William will know things we might not have heard. If not him, his best mate Joseph seems to be in possession of any news or rumours going round. Unfortunately, most of them always come true." Peg went over to get the milk from the aluminium can, which Annie had placed on the draining board. Sniffed it and made a face. "Uh, when did you buy the milk?"

"A few days ago. Has it gone off already? Give it to me, let me have a taste." Annie took the can and poured some into Peg's tea, which immediately curdled, took a look at it and poured the milk into a saucepan.

"I better boil it and maybe I can rescue it by adding a bit of sugar. George would go mad if he found out I just let it go sour." Annie shrugged her shoulders and continued, "Sometimes he gets real angry about little things like that, says he will shorten my housekeeping if I continue wasting things."

Annie ignored the questing look her sister shot at her. "Why have we been told to evacuate our children anyway? I thought Chamberlain promised 'Peace in our Time'?"

Chapter 28

1 September 1939

Annie had been told to stay at home. But she wanted to see her nieces and nephews going off. She hoped Peg and Kate knew what they were doing. The noise at Liverpool Lime Street Station was deafening when she got there. She had not imagined it would be that crowded. No way would she be able to spot her family here. What did she think she would achieve coming here anyway? Try and change their minds? Shouting their names would not help, you could hardly hear yourself think.

"Jesus, Annie, I told you this is a daft idea. We'll never find them. Oi, you, stop pushing," Flo shouted on top of her voice and angrily shoved a man out of the way.

He shot around, then he saw Annie's swollen belly, tipped his cap with his fingertips, "Sorry, missus, just trying to find my kids."

Flo shrugged her shoulders, pointing to her ears.

"I just got here in time before the train leaves, could not get away from the docks early, although I had booked the time off," he shouted back.

"How are we going to find anybody here at all, there must be easily a thousand kids plus families, I reckon."

"Are your kids going?" The man tried to make himself heard all the while pushing his way forward, leaving space for them to follow.

"No, not ours, but some of the family, I think we will have to give up looking."

"No way," shouted Annie. "Let's at least try."

"Mammy, Mammy! Where are you! Mammy."

The little girl right in front of Flo stopped.

"Have you seen my mammy, I can't find her."

Tears streamed down her face, tears now smeared with snot from her nose and dirt from her fingers, where she had unsuccessfully tried to clean her face. She had grabbed Flo by the coat. Flo was just about to bend down and pick her up, when Annie pulled her arm back.

"No!"

"What?" Annie pointed to her head and then indicated towards the girl. The girl's head was alive with lice. Now Flo saw the state this little girl was in. Boots without laces, no socks, a short checked dress, no coat, no jacket, a small pillowcase hanging loosely by her side. A brown paper bag, a label around her neck showing her name. A gas mask fastened with a string around her tiny waist.

"There you are, stop running away. Sorry, Miss. I hope she did not bother you." A larger girl now got hold of her, and they disappeared into the crowd.

"Which train are you looking for?" The man had turned round and faced them again.

"To be honest, we have no idea, we should not have come. They told us not to. But Annie here, she never listens."

"Wales, I think, they are going somewhere in Wales."

"All the trains go to Wales, love."

"What about your kids?"

"Wales." He now smiled. "Okay, let's look for 'the' train to Wales. Give me your pushchair."

"No!" He was surprised by Annie's reaction, raised his eyebrows and gave her a questioning look.

"No, thank you, the pushchair helps to keep me steady." Annie was sorry the way she had reacted, all the man had done was try to help them.

"Annie, Annie." Flo looked behind her when she realised Annie was no longer following her. She turned round, and

Annie has disappeared somewhere in the crowd. "Annie!" She kept on shouting, trying to push her way back.

"Sorry, sorry, looking for my friend, she was here only a second ago."

"We are all looking for somebody," a woman screamed hysterically. "Stop trying to jump the queue."

"There is a woman lying on the floor," shouted another. "Ambulance, I need an ambulance."

Chapter 29

"Mam? Mam?" Dorothy had crawled out from underneath the bed her dad had insisted she hid beneath with her brother and sister.

"Dorothy, do as you are told and get back under the bed and don't make a noise," her dad whispered.

"But I am scared, I want my mam." She started crying.

"For goodness sake, Dorothy, stop crying, we have been told no lights and no noise."

"Who told us, Dad?" Now it was Jeffrey who came sliding out from underneath.

"Yes, Dad, who?" Grace decided to take charge and pushed Dorothy back under, she was the eldest after all, and if somebody needed to find out, it was her. She was not going to be pushed around by her younger brother and sister.

"I want my mam," Dorothy whimpered again. "Dorothy!" It was Grace who raised her voice.

"You know Mam is in the Liverpool infirmary because she did not feel well. Aunty Flo took her there. They took Derek with them. You are not helping your mam by being a cry baby." Grace's words shot in Dorothy's direction.

"But it has gone dark and we have no lights, they have all gone out. Look!"

There was nothing stopping Dorothy now. She wiggled herself free from her brother's grasp and ran to the window. She banged her leg on the chair holding their clothes, which fell over with a loud crash, scattering everything on to the floor. George jumped up from his place on the floor he had sat on, leaning with his back against the wall. He was at Dorothy's side in two large steps. Dorothy held her arm over her head, trying to protect it from any possible slap, which most likely would follow. But instead of feeling pain, she felt her father's arm around her and his hands softly stroking her face.

Grace joined her dad and Dorothy at the window. Jeffrey was not to be outdone and tried to wiggle himself clear of the spring, which had attached itself to his sweater. He gave it a short pull, and he heard the fabric rip. His mam would be furious, she only gave it to him a week ago. She was so proud she found it at the clothes sale at the church.

"Dad, can I put the curtain to the side, just a little bit?"

This time it was Grace who decided to push her luck. She did not wait for her father to reply and parted the curtains in the middle. Total darkness outside. Not one light. Not even a glimmer from the docks or the match works, no glow of a cigarette from the neighbour who used to smoke just outside. Nothing, just black. "I read a book at school, Dad, about the future, when everything went black. Is this the end of the world, Dad?" Jeffrey had pushed himself between Grace and Dorothy. "What is happening, Dad, why is everything black?"

George took a deep breath and sighed, "I don't know whether this is the end of the world, son, but what I do know is that Hitler has today attacked Poland, and it might as well be the end of the world."

Chapter 30

3 September 1939

Silence. All faces pointed towards the bar at the other end of the pub. The landlord was on top of a small ladder, twiddling with the sound button on the wireless he had installed some months before.

> This morning the British Ambassador in Berlin handed a final note stating that unless we hear from them by 11 o'clock that they were prepared at once to withdraw their troops from Poland, a state of war would exist between us. I have to tell you now that no such undertaking has been received and consequently, this country is at war with Germany.

Now everybody spoke at once. George tried to make himself heard, but Kieran just shook his head and pointed to his ears. Then he indicated with his hand to drink up and pointed his head towards the door. They fought their way through a crowd of men, which had pushed forward and stared at the radio whilst shouting to the landlord to put the sound up. Like it was his fault that no further announcements were made. Others pushed George and Kieran to one side, trying to be the first out of the door. "Oi," was all George managed to say, before he recognised one of his workmates.

"Sorry, George, I have to get home, my little ones are being evacuated today, on one of those big boats, travelling all the way to Canada." When he saw George's questioning look, he continued, "My sister, you know my sister. She emigrated to Canada with her new fella last year and we got a telegram to send our youngest. Mind you, we are sending all of them. We have not told her that, no time you see." And with that he disappeared amongst a group of men and women now gathered outside. Some of them wondering what the rush was and why people kept running and pushing. A red-haired woman, looking a little familiar to George, pushing a pram, now stopped in from of them.

"I should have gone, do you think it is too late for that now? Will they have any more places in the countryside for me and the kid? I am a good worker, you see."

With that, she pushed her jumper up to expose her arm.

"Muscles, look I am strong, I can work in the fields. Please tell them to take me on the next train, me and my baby." She held Kieran by the sleeve. "You look official, please tell them. I don't want to be here when the bombs fall. They will bomb us now, don't you think?"

Several other people had now formed a circle around George and Kieran.

"Yes, what do you think that Hitler bloke will do?" shouted a man from the back.

Kieran put his hands up, trying to silence the gathering. "Look mates, I am only a seaman, and this here is my mate, a dockworker. We have no idea, we just found out Britain is at war, same as you did. Now let us get through, we have to see to our own families." Nobody moved. "Do what we do – go home."

Slowly the people turned away and went off into a different directions. George and Kieran stood there, rooted to the ground.

"She is right, you know, I should have listened to Peg and let Annie and the children go. They would be safe there, somewhere in the country, protected from what is bound to happen now. I was selfish, I did not let them go."

Chapter 31

"Wake up, Annie. You did well. Here he is, a boy, you have a beautiful baby boy." The doctor leaned over Annie, shining a small torch into her eyes.

"How long has she been like that?" He directed his question to Flo who sat next to Annie on a small wooden stool. She had sat there since the baby was born, holding Annie's hand. Occasionally, she stood up and mopped Annie's forehead, which felt far too hot.

"She has not woken once, doctor," Flo told him.

"Nurse, take the baby back and call me if there is any change."

Earlier in the day, Flo dropped little Derek off at Annie's neighbour before she went back to the hospital, hoping Annie would give birth soon. The foreman at work had been very understanding. He was a father himself and besides, he liked Annie and her family. He felt sorry for her that Annie had not been able to safely evacuate her children. That George has a lot to answer for, he often thought. He would get Annie a cleaning job here if he could. Money must be tight in that household and now yet another child on the way. Flo would not get paid of course but at least he was able to keep her job open until she came back. He'd rather let somebody else go first before Flo would lose her job. She was one of the best workers and he was glad that Annie persuaded him to let Flo replace her when she left to have her first child. How many years ago was that? He had quite a problem at that time to calm the other woman, who was sure that job was hers. Well he had been right. He saw her the other day all posh at the arm of an old bloke in expensive clothes. She totally ignored him when he lifted his hat to greet her. Obviously she did not want this fella to know she was working class, like everybody else.

Annie blinked and slowly opened her eyes.

"Doctor, she is opening her eyes." Flo jumped off her stool and was at the end of the ward before the doctor disappeared. She held him by his arm.

"It's Annie, doctor, come and see, she just woke up, I told you she would be alright."

"Nurse, bring the baby back."

"Annie, there you are, how are you feeling? You gave us quite a fright. Look, here is your baby boy." With that, he took the infant from the nurse's arm and gave him to Annie. Annie moved his blanket away from his face to take a first look at her son. Yes, the doctor was right, he was beautiful. A mass of dark hair framed his delicate features.

"What are you going to name him, Annie?"

"We have not thought about it yet."

"I would name him David. Yes, Annie, if he were my little boy, I would name him David," said the doctor and stroked the little boy gently across his head.

Chapter 32

Garston, Liverpool – January 1940

Loud banging against the front door. Annie did not have the strength to leave the bed and go to open it. Grace's head appeared from underneath a coat she used for extra cover over the flimsy blankets.

"Grace, put the coat back over, don't let the freezing air in," protested Dorothy, trying to slide further towards her mother's body in the hope she would warm up.

"Be careful, Dorothy, mind Derek and the baby," Annie managed to say without stopping, blowing on her cold hands in a futile attempt to stop new frostbites on her fingers.

"Jeffrey, Jeffrey, go and have a look who is at the door."

"But, Mam!"

"I'll go, as usual." Grace was out of the bed already. Still fully clothed and wearing her shoes. Nobody had taken any of their clothes off for the last two days.

"Just make sure that you keep Derek warm, he has already got a fever and we can't afford a doctor," Grace continued; she was already wise for such a young age. She had learned some time ago her younger siblings depended on her wit and resourcefulness at critical moments. Especially since their mam had been unwell. Mam still hadn't fully recovered from giving birth to our David, she thought.

Grace opened the front door only about one inch, her mother told her not to let anybody into their flat who she did not recognise. Flo pushed against the door with her back. She entered the hallway backwards pulling a basket. The contents of the basket left black smudges on the otherwise clean linoleum.

"Jesus, it's freezing in here, almost as cold as outside." She took her gloves off and rubbed her hands, then shook them to get some blood flowing through them.

"Where is your mam? And why are you not at school?" she shouted after Grace who had run back into their bedroom and tried to get herself under the blanket. But Dorothy was going to have none of it.

"Get off, it is my turn to have the coat, get lost...Mam!"

"Get out of bed, all of you, no not you, Annie, wait until we made a fire in the kitchen."

"Aunty Flo, we don't have any coal, and Dad chopped up a chest for firewood. See, there are all the baby clothes and nappies stored over there. That is where the chest was. But that firewood is now gone, and Dad says we can't chop up any more furniture. Who knows when he can find some plywood to rebuild the things he has already used for keeping his family warm," he said. Dorothy rumbled on, holding Flo around her waist, hoping she would open her coat and let her slip under it and hold her close.

"There is no school today," added Grace, just remembering that Flo had asked her what she was doing at home.

"They don't have any wood to heat the large boiler they said, do you think they could chop up the desks?"

Dorothy hoped they would, she did not like going there, she wanted to be with her mam. She had heard them say that bombs might fall on Liverpool soon. She did not know what that actually meant, but it sounded really scary. What if the bombs fell from the sky when she was at school, and her mother could not come to get her? No, I hope they chop up the desks and chairs, and then we have nowhere to sit. Surely, they would not make us sit on the floor, she thought. I'd better ask Aunty Flo. Aunty Flo always knows everything.

"Dorothy, go and help Jeffrey to take the basket into the kitchen."

Dorothy was back within seconds, "Mam, Mam, we have wood and coal! Aunty Flo brought it, look." With that, she held two lumps of coal towards her mother.

"Flo, where on earth did you get them from?" Annie now livened up.

"Me and several others went to the railway line yesterday. We had heard that the match works were getting a delivery of coal during the night. We hid in the undergrowth. Waited for hours, bloody freezing in the ice storm, I can tell you."

For once, Annie did not mind the bad language in front of the children and climbed out of bed.

"No, you stay, Annie, we'll just make the fire. Anyway, the train finally arrived. Most of us crawled on our bellies to the carriages. It was really difficult, pulling baskets, buckets and sacks. Anything we could take. Some of us stayed behind as lookouts. Two managed to climb on top of the wagons and threw down the coal. The rest of us collected it as fast as we could. Then we legged it. There is another load coming next week. We will be better organised by then."

Now Flo laughed. "As Kieran says, 'The luck of the Irish'."

"Mam, shall I make some tea?" Grace shouted from the kitchen, already filling the kettle.

"Yes, I will use the old teabags from yesterday, and yes, I will not fill the kettle too full so that I do not waste any gas, and yes, I know Dad has only put a shilling into the meter," she said more to herself, then out loud.

When they sat around the kitchen table in a slowly warming kitchen, they dared to take their coats off. "Oh, look what I found." Flo reached into her large coat pocket and produced a packet of garibaldi biscuits.

"Aunty Flo, are we allowed to have one?" Dorothy had climbed on to Flo's lap, hoping her aunty would stay for a while. Mam was always in a much better mood when Flo was here.

"You managed to get biscuits?" Annie had turned round from facing the fire, pulling little David close to her chest, feeding him his much overdue feed. My lovely little son, he is such a good boy, he never cries, just looks at me with his dark brown eyes. There is some Irish in you my beautiful boy, yes, just look at your dark hair. Just like your mam, she thought. His tiny hands balled into fists, in defiance to the rest of the world. Yes, my little one, don't give in. She kissed him softly on his forehead. She was brought back out of her thoughts by Flo.

"They are not rationed yet. That's reminds me, Annie, did you get all the identity cards and the ration books for the children?"

"What are ration books?" asked Dorothy, happily sucking on her treat to make it last as long as possible.

"It is something with your name on, so we can get some food, Thicko."

"Mam, Jeffrey is calling me names again."

"Jeffrey, apologise to your sister." When he did not say anything, Grace said, "Don't worry, Dorothy – wait until I tell Dad about it tonight."

The prospect of a very tired and cold Dad hearing about him calling his sister names certainly changed things immediately.

"Sorry, Dorothy."

"Yes, we got all the cards, but we still need the stamps from the shop, so they can put us on their rations list. George will go past there on his way home today."

Chapter 33

June 1940

"Did Bob get his call-up for military service?"

Annie had taken Derek and David over to Peg's house. She wanted to borrow five shillings. Grace needed a pair of shoes and some new clothes. She was outgrowing everything at the moment and had passed on most of her things to her younger sister. Annie had heard there was going to be a very large rummage sale this Saturday. Flo was helping out at the church hall where it would take place. Flo had already managed to 'lift' a few things for the boys, but the warden in charge now kept a very close eye on her. However, Flo had persuaded her to let Annie come early since she was a 'family' member.

"No, they are only drafting men between the ages of nineteen to twenty-seven years of age. And in any case, he has been transferred to work in Fazakerley."

"Fazakerley? But that is miles away. What is so important that he has to go all the way to Fazakerley?"

"If he works there, he might not get drafted at all. I certainly do not want him to go to war. You have heard about the British retreat over in France, haven't you?"

"Which retreat from France? I did not even know we are fighting over there."

"Here, read it for yourself." Peg threw the newspaper Bob had brought home the previous evening on to the kitchen table.

British defeat in France. Over 300,000 troops rescued by our heroic fleet of volunteers, who went into action as soon as it was known that our brave troops were trapped. Thousands of vessels, some large, some little, some only being able to rescue a single person. They all went across the Channel, over to Dunkirk, to bring our boys home. After several days, the rescue mission is now completed. It is with great sadness that we have to announce the loss of some of our brave men. Prime Minister Churchill promised retaliation for this atrocity. In his speech in the House of Commons, he stated "We shall fight on the beaches, we shall fight on the landing grounds, we shall fight in the fields and in the streets, we shall fight in the hills, we shall never surrender."

"Oh, my God." Annie put the paper down. "Anybody we know?"

"I hope not, but that is why I am happy that Bob now works at the Royal Ordnance Factory in Fazakerley. They need skilled men like our Bob."

"What happens in Fazakerley?"

"They make rifles and guns. That is all Bob would tell me. It must be an important job because he is one of very few people who are collected at the end of the road."

"Every morning?"

"He will have to work shifts because he has to train some new people. Some of them are women."

"Women? Women in a gun factory? What would their jobs be?" Annie was totally puzzled. She never imagined women would work next to men doing similar jobs.

"With all the men going to war, there would be nobody else to do the work, would there?"

Peg bent down towards the kitchen floor and gave Derek a small slice of cake she had baked yesterday.

"Here, Annie, have another piece, you look like you need it. You look far too pale for my liking."

"Thanks Peg, how did you manage to make this cake

so delicious? My cake hardly ever has any sugar in it. It is precious in our house since it has been rationed."

"Yes, same here. I had some syrup left. I used a bit of that and egg powder. Things are difficult to get, especially since I need to hand over extra ration coupons to the school to make sure our children get a proper meal. Wherever they are," she added more quietly.

"Have you still not heard from them?"

Peg shook her head.

"But they have been gone for months now. Surely somebody at the school can tell you where they live and whether they managed to find a place together. You are allowed to visit them, you know. What did the headmaster tell you when you asked last time?"

"Always, the same. They are sure that they are well and in good families. They have heard only twice from the teacher who confirmed all children have found places. He could not be more specific than that."

"What town? Did he tell you what town they are in?"

"No, but he has more families in the same position we are in, and he is doing his best in difficult circumstances."

"What about our Kate's kids. Where are they?"

"They are coming home."

"What? They are coming home, why, after all the drama sending them in the first place?"

"Kate finally managed to persuade William that home was the best place for them. Especially since no bombs have fallen on Liverpool at all. Quite a few people now believe this will not happen and that evacuating children and young families was a rash decision."

"And William agreed?"

"He must have because he got Kate a train ticket to go and collect them."

Chapter 34

RAF Martlesham – 10 July 1940

"Squadron, the day we have been preparing for has arrived. We got word from RAF Hawkinge that enemy planes have been spotted over the English Channel. Ships have come under attack. Our orders are to assist Squadron 54 from RAF Rochford and Squadrons 610 and 604 from RAF Gravesend. RAF Detling has been made available should the need arise to land closer than your own base. We will beat the German Luftwaffe at their own game and use the element of surprise. The weather is on our side. You have the capability to fly above the clouds and attack the enemy planes when they least expect it. This will be the battle for our freedom. The safety of our citizens now depends on you. Prepare to leave in groups of eight. All crew report to their station now. Safe flights and safe return. God be with you."

William and Joseph were ready. The first ones out of the hangar. Scanning the sky as they went.

"Gunner Winfield, you are with me." One of the fighter pilots grabbed him by the arm. William had just a fraction of a second to look back at Joseph and then hurried to the last plane in line.

"Corporal McGreavy. Over there, man. Get back to the tower and radio control. Contact Hawkinge. It's Go! Go! Go!"

Sirens now started blaring and Joseph only half understood Squadron Leader Dorkin's instructions who had disappeared into the crowd of RAF pilots and gunners ready for the take-off.

"You come back safely, William, you hear!" He shouted after them. Knowing full well he could not be heard. The first of the planes roared over him. He counted and waited till the last plane had disappeared from sight. That was the one his friend would be in, sitting at the rear, a tight grip on the gun, making sure the turret did not swing out of control. He would be concentrating on nothing else. Joseph knew, because they had talked lot about this moment.

"McGreavy!" He was brought out of his thoughts by shouts from behind him and hurried up the staircase.

"Martlesham Control to Hawkinge! Martlesham Control to Hawkinge – planes airborne."

"Roger that."

"Hawkinge Control to Martlesham – enemy attack on Portsmouth Harbour! Repeat attack on Portsmouth Harbour confirmed."

"Roger that."

"Martlesham Control to Hawkinge – require damage report."

"Hawkinge Control to Martlesham – awaiting report."

"Look out, look out! Martlesham Control to Hawkinge! We have enemy aircraft approaching!"

"Martlesham, Martlesham, come in Martlesham."

"Martlesham, come in Martlesham."

"Attack, attack, we are under attack."

"Everybody to their station, hurry, hurry. McGreavy stay with radio control."

Joseph's chair had tumbled backwards from the fall-out of the blast on the ground. The tower shook. He tried to scramble back up, but only managed to lift himself high enough to look out of the broken window. Smoke from the left of the airfield started drifting into the tower. More aircraft noises coming from above.

"Get the anti-aircraft guns into position! Now!" He heard from below him, followed by, "Wait. Wait, these are our own aircrafts! Our boys are coming back."

He was not sure whether his orders were to remain where he was. He turned to where the radio controls should be, but all the instruments where now covered by broken glass. He started brushing it off with his elbow whilst still kneeling on the floor. He hoped to re-establish a connection and tried to feel for the mike. He pressed the button and put the microphone close to his mouth.

"Martlesham to Hawkinge. Come in Hawkinge."

Nothing, not even static. The line was dead. He crawled underneath to see whether a connection had come loose when the building shook. He found a cable under a large sheath of glass. The cable was cut straight through.

Somebody tried to pull the door open behind him, but the door seemed stuck shut.

"Oi, give me a hand," he heard from the other side. Then heavy boots running in various directions, a large bang and the door flew open.

"Bloody hell! What happened here? We leave you lot alone for one moment, and the place is a shambles." William was now by his side and helped him get up.

"Did you get them?"

"Oh, yes, we got those buggers."

Chapter 35

"George, wake up, wake up. The sirens are going."

"Go back to sleep, Annie, it's a false alarm again, or the all clear." George pulled the blanket back over his head.

"George, I can hear noises on the stairs, everybody is up. We have to go, come on."

"In a minute." George went further down under the covers.

"Grace, Jeffrey, Dorothy, the sirens are going, quick, quick, get up, get dressed and don't forget your gas masks. Run downstairs to the air-raid shelter." Annie was shouting whilst taking Derek from his bed.

"Grace, take David from the cot and wrap him in his blanket. For goodness sake, do not drop him."

"I can't see, Mam. Dorothy, ouch, watch where you are going."

"Mam, I am scared."

"It's alright Dorothy. Jeffrey, take Dorothy's hand."

"What?"

Annie tried to adjust her eyes to find some movement in the darkness of the room. The black fabric covering the windows gave the inside of the flat an eerie stillness in spite of the commotion the children made. Annie touched a wall with one hand, trying to feel the way out of the bedroom to the hallway and the front door. Derek on her arm. He felt hot. A strange sensation of heat filtered through her coat and nightdress underneath. She took her gas mask, and felt Grace and Jeffrey, behind her. Annie noticed Dorothy at her side, Dorothy never let her out of her sight these days.

Always afraid. Annie opened the door.

"Annie, hurry, you are the last ones to leave." John from the apartment on the first floor of their block was the warden. It was his job to make sure everybody was out and down in the shelter when the alarm sounded.

"Is it a false alarm again?"

"This one is for real, Annie. Grace, give me your David. Come on you, hurry along now."

"I can't see anything."

"Yes we can, look."

A flush of bright light through the corridor window. They stopped in their tracks. The light was followed by an ear-splitting noise, and the building seemed to move.

"Mam!"

"Hurry, hurry, hurry, to the shelter, now!" shouted the warden. Jeffrey and Grace ran past Annie and were already out of the door. Dorothy still clinging to her mam. Outside on the right side, a fire was burning. The heat made Annie take a step back. She covered her mouth with her hand, trying to avoid choking.

"Dorothy. Run!" She managed to shout before she started to cough.

Aircraft noises drowned out Annie's instructions. She hurried after Dorothy. A whistling sound, silence, then a massive boom, which seemed to be really close by. The earth shook under her feet, and Annie fell to the ground, dropping Derek when she fell.

"Derek!"

Nobody heard Annie's cry for help. She was alone, laying on the ground, unable to move. From fear or shock, she did not know, but her legs refused to carry her weight. There was burning rubble near to where Derek had fallen. He managed to get up by himself. Covered in dirt, he toddled over to where she lay. He did not cry, just sat on the ground next to Annie. The planes came back. She imagined them to be somewhere right above her in the dark sky. She pulled Derek over by his arm. And covered him with her body as best she could. One arm over Derek and with the other shielding her head. Noises, threatening noises. Deafening sounds. The earth underneath would not keep still. And hot, so hot. My children, I hope they are safe. She must have said it out loud. She felt somebody pulling her at the back of the coat.

"Thank God I found you. I thought you were with the rest inside. Come on, Annie. Let's get you out of here."

She could only hear some of what the warden had said. I must have gone deaf, she thought. The only light as far as she could make out were burning fires. She looked up and saw Derek in the safe arms of the warden. And then felt his hand giving her a final pull up.

A dim light was on inside the shelter, and several candles were flickering. Annie spotted Grace and Dorothy at one of the sides, sitting on the floor next to Grace's friend, Joan. Joan's mother had David on her lap. From where Annie was standing, she could see David was fast asleep. Nobody spoke. Joan's mother waved to her to come over and moved to the side to make space for Annie. The warden handed Derek back to her, and Annie made her way across.

"Where have you been? We have been here for ages. Did the tenements get hit? What about the match works?"

"I did not see anything – just tried to get here as soon as I could."

"Derek? Oh, my God! Derek!"

"Mam, Mam, what is it?" Grace tried to make her way over. "Mam, what is the matter with our Derek? Mam! He is shaking. Please make it stop. Mam!"

"Derek, Derek!" Derek was shaking uncontrollably, thrashing his arms and legs. Moving his head from side to side. His body bucked.

"Grace, get the doctor, run as fast as you can." Grace

stood still for only a fraction, turned around and headed for the door.

The neighbours had formed a circle around Annie and Derek who was now lying on the floor. Two of her neighbours were already on their knees, one holding his arms and one holding on to his legs. A third neighbour had taken a cloth and wet it with cold water. She was now dampening the sweat off Derek's forehead. Annie stroked his cheeks gently with her hand.

"Derek, wake up Derek, your mam is here." Derek's body started to relax and then he was totally still. Annie bent over his tiny body.

"Derek, oh no, not my Derek." Annie rocked back and forth, now holding his lifeless body in her arms. Jeffrey had fought his way to the centre of the circle and put his hand on his mam's shoulder.

"Mam, where is our dad?"

Chapter 36

As soon as the 'all clear' was given, they went back upstairs. The neighbours had followed them wordlessly into the hall of the tenement. Nobody went into their own place. Most women were crying quietly. Men, women and children remained standing on the staircase, long after Annie and her family had closed their door. It was starting to get light outside, but the flat was in total darkness. Jeffrey had opened the door with the key he always carried on a string around his neck, tucked in under his sweater he wore most days. Although this year, late into August, it was still very hot. He envied some of his friends who most of the time played outside in their undershirts. But his mam never allowed them to go out like that.

Annie did not let anybody take Derek off her. She hardly noticed his weight. Grace walked ahead, carrying David, who had started to wriggle. Grace used all her strength not to drop him. Dorothy went for the light switch and the lights came on.

"Switch that bloody light off," they heard George shout from the bedroom. He opened the bedroom door, and he stood in front of them in his pyjama bottoms.

"What is going on?"

Annie walked past him with Derek in her arms, went over to the bed and put him down. Then she climbed into bed and laid her body next to his. She took the bedcover and pulled it over both of them.

"Hush, little baby don't you cry, mama's gonna sing you a lullaby." They heard Annie's soft voice.

"Bloody hell, will somebody tell me what is going on?" George now bellowed, looking from one to the other.

"It's our Derek, he is dead."

"No Annie, that can't be true? What happened? Tell me, Annie, for God's sake, speak to me, woman."

"Where were you, George? Where were you when our children needed their father?"

"Annie, please! Please let me take Derek, let me look at him. Did he get hit, what happened? For goodness sake, tell me."

George was kneeling in front of the bed, his right arm resting on the mattress, his body shaking, tears streaming down his face.

"I'll kill those bloody Germans, you wait and see. I'll kill them with my bare hands."

"It wasn't the German bombs that killed our Derek."

"It wasn't? What happened?"

"Our Derek was ill, George, and we did not even know. He lost his life in a dark crowded air-raid shelter with only his mam and brothers and sisters besides him. He was comforted by strangers, George. Why weren't you there, George? Why weren't you there for your little boy?"

George pushed himself off the bed, walked silently across to where the chair stood. Threw all the clothes off until he found his trousers and work shirt. He got dressed, and walked out of the room past Grace, Jeffrey and Dorothy who had watched their parents from the doorway. Taking his cap off the rack, he opened the front door and without saying a word, he left.

Chapter 37

Three nights, the bombs rained down on Liverpool. Three days Annie was wondering where George was. Three nights she was comforting her children in the air-raid shelter. Grace had gone to get Peg and Flo the day after Derek died. Dorothy stayed with her mother most of the time. She screamed when she woke from a brief sleep. Jeffrey, nearly ten years old, had taken over the responsibility of a man. He thrived in his new found freedom. He went to the undertakers and told them to come to his home. At first, they did not believe him and told him to bring his mam. He returned later with a note his mam wrote. The undertaker felt really guilty that he did not go with the boy in the first place and gave him a sweet. Jeffrey licked it a couple of times then put it into his trouser pocket for later. His mam trusted him with the ration book. The neighbours had collected money for them. Everyone gave as much as they could for the burial, they said. He made sure some of the money was put aside for the gas meter. He hid it under the bed in his box where he kept his cigarette cards and marbles. He had heard his parents argue about money some evenings. His mother begging for more, but his dad not giving her any. He knew his mother had to borrow, mainly from Aunty Flo. Especially now, since his mam had lost her cleaning job at the Co-op. They said they could no longer afford it, now with the war and all that. Grace persuaded Dorothy to help her to keep the kitchen as clean as she could for the constant flow of people coming and going. Each night, they raced down to the shelter. Derek's body was still in Annie's bedroom. She had by now washed him gently and put him in his best clothes. The clothes she got from Flo, last time there was a rummage sale at the church. They looked so new, and Annie had wanted to save them for Christmas when they had made plans to all meet at Peg's house. Arrangements had been made for them to sleep over. There was enough space shared out between Peg and Kate's houses with Peg's children tucked away safely somewhere in the country. Annie had readily agreed to this. It would be nice for her children, and she quietly worried about Peg. She did not want Peg and Bob to sit there all by themselves.

George returned the day of Derek's funeral, carrying a small white coffin he had made in the workshop at the docks. He looked unwashed and unshaven. He pulled the bath from the store cupboard into the kitchen. Then watched by his bewildered children, he started to fill the kettle and lit the gas stove. He filled the bath with several kettles of boiled water. Added cold water, got a towel from the cloth rack above the stove, closed the kitchen door, dropped his clothes on the floor and climbed into the bath. When he was washed and dried, he shouted for Grace to bring him some clean clothes, never bothered shaving. He went back into the hall, took the coffin and went into the bedroom. Annie stood next to a small coffin the undertaker had placed on the floor.

George gently lifted Derek out. And cradled him in his arms.

"Give me that," he nodded with his head towards the bed where Annie had placed Derek's light blue blanket. George wrapped it around the small body and lowered Derek into the coffin he had made.

"No child of mine is going to be buried in a stranger's coffin," he said, turning his head to Annie. He knelt on the floor and remained there until Peg, Bob and Kate arrived.

"It's time to go, Annie," was all Bob said.

George stood up, took Annie's hand. Annie looked at him with her sad dark brown eyes and pulled her hand away. George lifted the coffin, carried it in front of him, with both arms underneath. He was the first one in the line, followed by Annie, their children, Peg, Bob and Kate. Silently they walked down the staircase where the neighbours stood, waiting to accompany Derek on his last journey.

Chapter 38

"Aunty Kate, what is Uncle William and that man doing in your garden?"

"They are building an air-raid shelter."

"An air-raid shelter? Are you going to have your own air-raid shelter in your back garden?"

"Yes, your uncle says, now with your cousins back home and him away fighting in the war most of the time, we need our own shelter. He wanted to be sure we are safe."

"Can I go and have a look."

"Of course, but don't be in the way. Leave your bag here."

"Hello young Jeffrey, are you here to help us?"

"No, Uncle William, my mam sent me for the apples Aunty Peg said we could have. I'll go and pick the fallen ones off the ground as soon as Aunty Peg is back home."

"Where has Peg gone, then?"

"To get the sugar. I gave her our ration cards because they did not have sugar left at the Co-op where we live. It is much nicer living here, isn't it, Uncle William?"

"Maybe one day you could all come and live over here at Stamfordham Drive."

"Do you think so, Uncle William? Do you really think we will ever live in a house like yours?"

"Joseph, you remember Annie's Jeffrey, don't you."

"Hello, Jeffrey. My goodness you have grown. You turned into a fine young man. Do you think you could give us a hand whilst your Aunty Peg is still out?"

"Am I really allowed to help with building an air-raid shelter?"

"Sure you are, we want it to be ready before we leave."

"Are you fighting the Germans, like my Uncle William?"

"Yes, young man. Now take the shovel from over there and start digging along the line we have marked out. See the pegs and string? Dig in a line just in front of it, that wide, see? Joseph showed him a brick, which he had picked from the top of the coal storage.

Jeffrey nodded at his uncle's friend, Joseph. He remembered Joseph from the time when they first moved into the tenements, although he was a small boy then. He picked up the shovel and dug as hard as he could. The three of them worked wordlessly for a while until Jeffrey asked, "Uncle William, how deep should I dig?"

"It has to be at least up to your knee," replied his uncle fixing a sheet of corrugated iron, which was curved at the top.

"Damn!" said his uncle, the pliers had slipped and cut his hand. He looked at the damage to his palm. "Kate!" he shouted and disappeared back into the kitchen, leaving drops of blood on the path.

Jeffrey took this as a sign to stop for a while, and checked his hands for any signs of blisters.

"Uncle Joseph, what will the shelter look like?"

Joseph stopped attaching bolts to both sides of a metal door, which was leaning against the fence.

"See the sheets of corrugated iron your uncle showed you?" Jeffrey nodded. "Well, both ends are going to be fixed in the centre to form a kind of archway. The front and back of the shelter are standing there, at the wall, see?" Another nod. "We then have to bolt everything together, and that should be it."

"Will it be big enough for all of us?"

"Jeffrey, your Aunty Peg is back!" shouted William from the kitchen door.

"I have got to go, bye, Uncle Joseph."

"Bye, young Jeffrey, say hello to your mam and dad."

Chapter 39

Annie passed the last of the toffee apples out through the open window. "Sorry, Ricky, that was the last one. If I can get any more apples, you will be the first to know."

She saw the disappointed look on the boy's face, clutching his pennies in one hand and steadying himself against the wall with the other. She leaned out of the window and looked down to the floor. He was on tiptoes in his bare feet. Annie knew his mother had a difficult time coping and little Ricky was left all by himself most of the time. She had heard that his mother had been re-admitted to the institution only last week. Neighbours had seen her running down the corridor screaming the other night. It had been like that ever since she was notified that her two older children had perished when the City of Benares was torpedoed and sunk by a German submarine in the Atlantic – the ship that should have delivered her children to safety in Canada for Ricky's aunt to look after. They had heard on the wireless that no more children are going to be sent abroad. No consolation for a mother who had just lost hers. She knew the other kids from the tenement quite often teased little Ricky about the colour of his hair, which was bright red like his mother's. Kids could be cruel sometimes. She had warned hers, if she ever caught one of them calling little Ricky names, to expect a right hiding.

"Ricky, who is looking after you with your mam gone away?" The little boy just shrugged his shoulders.

"Why don't you come inside, I might find a glass of milk and a biscuit for you."

Annie was rewarded with a big smile and a nod. She pulled the kitchen window down as far as she could. It did not close properly anymore. She would have to ask George to take a look at it. The little bit of heat that was in their home would all but disappear through it, she thought. She looked at the clock in the kitchen. The children would be home from school soon and David was still sleeping. Flo had promised to come round after finishing her shift at the bottle works. Annie was desperate to find another job. Selling toffee apples gave her the odd shilling or two, but if you considered the money and ration coupons for the sugar, it was hardly worth it. She realised her real reason for doing this was it took her mind of Derek. The happy faces of the children who bought them off her seemed to ease the pain. But Christmas was approaching fast, and she had nothing to give her children. There was no point asking George for more money. These days he entered every penny in his book. It was no good pleading with him. When he occasionally relented, he would write down the amount he lent her and take it away when her next housekeeping was due. Annie knew he still owed his sister Beattie the money he had borrowed for Derek's funeral. The sister reminded them about it at every opportunity. I will not send Grace to her fish and chip shop again. Last time Beattie made such a fuss in front of all the people in the queue. Grace came back crying. It was not that Beattie was giving them anything for free, even though they were her closest relatives. Beattie had not changed one little bit from the first day Annie had met her. She hoped married life would mellow her, but she was still as mean as ever. George would not hear a bad word about her, mind you.

Chapter 40

"But why, Mam? Why can't we go to Aunty Peg's and Aunty Kate's for Christmas? Dad, tell Mam we should go. Please tell her, Dad."

"You heard your mam, we are not going."

"But why? You said if the bombs stop falling, we can go. And there was no bombing last night, was there? No bombs have fallen close to us, not since the night our Derek died."

All eyes turned towards Grace. It was the first time somebody had mentioned that night since his body had been laid to rest.

Jeffrey felt the tension in the room and came to Grace's rescue. "Mam, Grace is right, maybe the bombing has stopped altogether. It's possible that the Germans have given up."

"Yes, maybe they have, Dad do you think they have?"

Dorothy climbed on her father's knee. She still liked to do that sometimes, although most of the time she felt too big. After all, she had been going to school for quite a while now. She was clutching her letter in one hand and placed the other arm around her father's neck. It was the letter she had written to Father Christmas. Like each year, they were allowed to put the toy they most wanted in a letter. All of them would throw them in the fireplace the night before. They would watch the flames licking them and burning them to ash, and she would watch the rising smoke. This was the moment the letter went up for Father Christmas to read. How he could read them after they had burned, she did not know. To her amazement, every year in the morning, when they could not wait any longer and raced into the front room, there it was, the one present she had asked for, standing right underneath the stockings her dad helped them to nail to the mantelpiece. George saw the letter in Dorothy's hand.

"Yes, maybe the bombing has stopped, or Hitler is taking pity on us, it is Christmas after all. But still, we should listen to your mam."

"What about the air-raid shelter, our Jeffrey helped to build in Aunty Kate's garden? He said we would all fit in there, didn't you, Jeffrey?"

Annie had been to Peg's house the day before. George had already taken the toys he made for the children. Nobody knew whether William would be on home leave from the RAF. Annie had given Peg her ration coupons to use at her Co-op and the extra Christmas money from George. The sisters had agreed that Kate and Peg should do the shopping. There would have been no point in Annie trying to get a few things and then carry them all the way over to Stamfordham Drive – plus the worry she might not get any of the food they discussed on her list. Ration coupons did not guarantee it was actually available. Sometimes you had to queue for hours outside in the freezing cold or driving wind and rain only to be told at the end of the line, there was nothing left. Recently, the manager of the shop had increased his prices, and that just before Christmas. She did not even believe he was allowed to do that. But who would you be able to complain to? Plus if you did, you would most certainly be crossed off his list. It was almost impossible to get anything on 'tick' these days. He laughed when he said, 'who knows if you will be around to pay your bill'. If George knew what she was charged these days, he would be around there in no time. So best to say nothing and try to stretch the money she got from him even further. It had crossed her mind quite often that if it would not be for her best friend Flo, their kids would to have gone to bed hungry most days.

Annie relented, and the family went off to stay at Peg and Kate's. They left before it got dark on Christmas Eve. It was crisp and below freezing. At least there was no snow on the ground; otherwise, it would have been impossible to push the pram with their nightclothes plus extra blankets, the kids' Christmas stockings and David on top. She hoped he would not start protesting or trying to get up and fall out. He had been walking for over a month now and never stood still. An adventurous little chap you are, our David, she thought. She tried to wrap him up as warm as she could, but he kept taking his gloves and hat off. The ones that one of Flo's workmates had knitted from an old sweater Flo had unravelled for the wool. Flo might come to Peg's place as well, unless Kieran is back. She had not heard from him since he went on one of those Merchant Navy vessels at the beginning of October. Annie knew Flo should really spend her time with her own cousin, especially since both of them worked at the stall on the market today. It was becoming increasingly more difficult to find any customers for the trinkets they tried to sell. Flo's cousin had said today was their last day. She had got herself work in Kirby. They had produced munitions there since September, Flo had told her. Flo was asked to work there as well, but luckily there was still enough work at her place and since Flo had 'worked herself up the ladder' she had no intention of travelling all the way to Kirby. 'No thanks, I don't want anything to do with the war if I can help it – with Kieran already out there exposed to all the danger.' She had confided this to Annie on one of the very few moments they had managed to share a beer.

Chapter 41

"Aunty Flo, Father Christmas has been, come and have a look." Dorothy pulled Flo inside the front room. She had been in the kitchen putting the orange peel into the bin, just as her Aunty Peg had told her. She looked out of the window, willing it to snow and saw Flo coming up the road towards the front garden.

"Happy Christmas, Dorothy," said Flo as soon as she was in the hall, picking her up and swinging her around. "My, you are getting heavy."

"My mam says I am a big girl now." Was her reply and not giving Flo the chance to take her coat off she was already heading to the front room, pulling on Flo by the sleeve.

Grace and Jeffrey were playing on the floor in front of the fire. Shauna had little David on her lap, trying to feed him some leftover Christmas pudding, without much success. He kept turning his face away, and most of the sweet landed on the lino where an excited puppy licked as fast as it fell. Shauna's brother lifted the puppy into his arms. "We got a puppy for Christmas."

"Did you now?" Flo raised her eyebrows giving Kate a questioning look and tried to take her coat off without pulling Dorothy's hands away.

"Happy Christmas, everybody," she said, hugging Annie, Peg and Kate in turn then gave a quick hug to George and Bob, before returning her attention to the rest of the children who were looking at her expectantly.

"Look what Father Christmas left at my front door, I am sure he meant it for me to bring it along." With that

131

announcement, a noisy group of children shot up and were at her side before she had the chance to open the bag she had placed on the floor. "Stop pushing, Jeffrey," Grace gave her brother a shove in the side.

"Stop it yourself," he replied and elbowed her out of the way.

"Mam!"

"Stop it right there, you two, otherwise you are going to bed early, Christmas or not," George threatened them, sitting in the only armchair in the room. The puppy tottered over, not wanting to miss out on what was going on with the new visitor, but first had to relieve itself in front of Shauna who was still holding David. He had stretched out his little arms wanting to be picked up by his Aunty Flo. Bob, standing behind George's armchair, watched the excitement with amusement.

"Well you two, you wanted a puppy, the first thing you can do is clear up this mess."

"But!"

"No but about it, or the puppy goes back where it came from," added Kate.

That settled it, Shauna handed David back to Annie, both kids disappeared into the kitchen but not before shouting, "Wait for us, Aunty Flo."

"Quite a welcoming committee," said Flo, standing in the middle of the room with the contents of her bag untouched.

"What is a welcoming committee?" Dorothy had used her chance and wiggled herself right in front of Flo again, looking down at the bag. Hoping to spot what was inside.

"It's all of you lot, come here." Flo put her arm around the children and gave them a squeeze all the while looking at Annie who held David by his hands, stopping him from running away through the dog mess towards his favourite aunt.

"Hurry up, Shauna." Grace decided it was about time she interfered and went towards the kitchen to get her cousins.

"You will be quite useless in tidying up, Matthew. Here, let me get it." She took the bucket of water off him. Shauna carried the mop. Matthew did not believe his luck and hurried back into the front room before Grace would change her mind.

Grace acts far too grown up for a girl her age, Flo thought as she watched her cleaning the floor whilst everybody else looked on, not raising a finger to help.

"About time, Grace," said Jeffrey as soon as both girls came back after emptying the bucket at the end of the garden.

"As I was saying," Flo continued where she had left off. "I found these outside my front door this morning." She opened her bag and reached for eight little paper bags, handing one to each child.

"Chocolate money! Look, Mam, we have chocolate money."

"Is it real gold?"

"Mine says, 1899 Farthing."

"Look, there is a bird on it."

"Who are these others for, Aunty Flo?"

"Father Christmas sent them for your cousins who are away, and he wants your Aunty Peg to look after them until they come back home." Flo handed the remaining bags over. Peg wiped away a tear, and Bob put his arm around her shoulders and gave Flo a thankful look.

"It smells delicious in here."

"We had goose, and Mam made stuffing and we had Christmas pudding," Dorothy volunteered, looking up momentarily from the floor where she was now putting her doll into the wooden bed Father Christmas had brought. She had a fight with Jeffrey last night when he had teased her that letters in the fire at Aunty Peg's don't count. You had to sleep in your own home for him to find you. He had got into real trouble from his dad and was not allowed to have some bread with the fat from the goose Aunty Peg had already in the oven.

"Come and sit over here." Bob pushed a kitchen chair in Flo's direction. "Shauna, get Flo her food from the kitchen." When Shauna did not move, he added, "Now. And Matthew, take your dog outside, your mam told you the dog lives outside, once George finds the time to build a kennel."

"Flo, how did you manage to get all those chocolates?" Annie was curious.

"You'd be surprised what a bottle of rum can get you nowadays."

"Not that bottle Kieran gave you on his last visit?" Now George perked up, he had just nodded off in the armchair, but the mention of rum woke him abruptly.

"The same."

"A bloody shame. That's what I would say."

"There are some bottles of beer in my bag." She pushed the bag over towards George with her foot.

George bent down and got himself a bottle, then pushed the bag towards Annie who had let go of David and took the beer off George, picked up the bag from the floor and went into the kitchen. She returned with two open bottles and filled everybody's glasses.

"I see you brought your nightclothes, so you decided to stay after all."

"Are you sure it is still alright, Peg?"

"Don't be silly, of course it is."

"Any word from Kieran?"

Chapter 42

"Show me that letter again, Flo." George bent forward and reached over to the table where the letter now lay. The children had gone to bed. They all wanted to sleep together in the front room at Kate's house. Bob, Kate and Peg carried the blankets over and gave strict instructions not to run around, or to light the fire.

George went as far as saying, "One sound coming from the direction of the air-raid shelter, and we are off home!" The kids had asked on numerous occasions during the afternoon, to go and see the shelter. When that did not work, Jeffrey argued that if the sirens did go off after all and they had to run there quickly, surely it would be better they knew where it is.

"You already know where it is," Bob had told him. Jeffrey saw the pleading eyes of his sisters and gave it another shot.

"Yes, but Grace and Dorothy don't know where to run to, what if they get lost in the dark?"

"Lost in the back garden? Shauna, if the sirens go off, take Dorothy by the hand. Matthew, you look after Grace. There you are Jeffrey, we have it covered."

"But what if we all don't fit in?"

"That's enough, Jeffrey," George snapped. "We have heard enough from you over the last two days. I don't know what's got into you lately."

It is with regret that we have to inform you that your husband, Kieran McDowell, has been lost at sea. On

135

28 October, this year, Merchant vessel RMS Empress *of* *Britain has been attacked and sunk by a German U-boat* *in the Atlantic, seventy miles north-west of Ireland.* *Initial reports stated that the first attack by air did not* *cause the boat to sink but instead it was being towed* *to land. During that journey, the U-boat struck. The* *vessel was badly hit and sunk at once. Most of the crew* *and passengers took to the lifeboats beforehand and* *have been rescued by the destroyer* HMS Echo *and* ORP *Burza. But the skeleton crew, which had remained on* *board during the tow, perished. We are sorry to inform* *you that your husband is not one of the survivors.*

"Oh, Flo, I am so sorry, very, very sorry. Oh, Kieran…not Kieran." Annie had tried to hold it together and comfort her friend, but could no longer hold back her tears. The two friends clung to each other and wept.

Bob as white as a sheet, had gone to the cupboard, got out their best glasses and filled them with the whiskey he had saved for a special occasion. Never imagining the occasion would be the loss of a good friend.

"I can't believe you sat there all afternoon not saying a word and the letter was in your bag all the time."

"What could I do, George, tell me what? The children will have to be told soon enough. At least let them have Christmas. This war is none of their fault, is it?" Flo had turned her head away from Annie's shoulders where it had been resting and faced George.

"Kieran. No, God, not Kieran. Please don't let it be true. Kieran, oh, Kieran." George put his hands over his face, bent down, rocked back and forth in the armchair and wailed.

"Kieran, no, not Kieran." Then he turned angry.

"What has he done to deserve this? Kieran, you daft bugger, what were you thinking of? How are we supposed to go on without him? That's it. I am enlisting tomorrow.

William was right. We have got to give it to the bloody Germans."

"Don't be stupid, George. If somebody enlists, it should be me."

"Why should it be you?" Now Peg started shouting at Bob, "What makes you think it should be you?"

"Enough! Enough, all of you. Nobody is going to enlist. That won't bring Kieran back. He never wanted anything to do with that war, just like me. What has it got to do with us anyway? We are Irish, for God's sake. What are we doing? Why are we fighting somebody else's bloody war?"

Chapter 43

"Annie, will you come with me?"

"Flo, I would, but how can I?"

"The fares will be paid for, they told me that. The company has been really good to me."

"It's not just that, George said he will be fine, I should go, but what about the children?"

"We can take Dorothy and David with us."

"But what am I supposed to do with Grace and Jeffrey?"

"Your Peg will look after them. Won't she? It's not that she has to be there when they come back from school. And her house is pretty empty with her kids away."

"Alright, yes, I will come with you, of course. I would never let you do this on your own. You are my best friend, for God's sake."

"Jesus, Annie, you better watch your words. What will Father O'Conner say if he heard you taking the good Lord's name in vain." Flo smiled. "Did Peg get a letter from her kids?"

"No, she is still waiting, but now at least she knows where they are."

"Fancy them being put on a boat to Australia. How could there be such a mix up?"

"The authorities are still tight-lipped about it, but admitted there was a spelling mistake on the paperwork, and Peg's kids apparently did not say anything. Just went where they were told to go. Peg has gone over it again and again, where she could have possibly gone wrong. They were with their teachers when they left from Lime Street

Station. After that, it is all unclear."

"Did the teachers get the blame?"

"I think so, but all they said was that they lost sight of them with all the pushing and shuffling. And when they arrived in Wales, the billeter who had them on his list, could not find them."

"But surely, they needed a medical examination and passports?"

"Our Peg is beside herself with worry, and I have never seen Bob so furious before. He is demanding a passage on the next ship going out. He wants to bring them back."

"Can he do that?"

"Well, he is damn well trying and who can blame him? You know, Flo, I feel so awful, when I tried to talk our Peg out of taking part in the evacuation, I sort of joked and said, what if they get lost and get sent to Australia instead? It's like it is my fault."

"Now you are being silly, but maybe you are right in one thing, maybe we should not ask Peg to look after Grace and Jeffrey, she has enough on her plate."

"I will ask her anyway, it might take her mind of things. Plus, I would really love to come along. I am worried about being seasick again on the journey, mind you."

"I have some ginger, which I had asked the company to get, saying it would be for me, of course. It's quite long, this crossing, all the way to Belfast."

"You are sure we will be safe, aren't you? Belfast has been bombed again only a few days ago. It said so on the wireless. And how do we travel onwards?"

"Not on a lorry this time, Annie. We go by train all the way to Ballyshannon. It's a doddle, Annie."

Chapter 44

Ballyshannon, Ireland

"Mam, stop fussing, you are spoiling them."

"If I can't fuss over my own flesh and blood, what sort of granny would I be? You come here, my little one, oh, you do look like your Uncle Patrick when he was a baby, oh, yes, you do, you do." David happily gurgled, sitting on his grandmother's knee.

Dorothy turned her eyes to the ceiling and then back to her mother. Annie laughed and shrugged her shoulders. It was so good to wake up in her old room back home. The kitchen still smelled of last night's dinner, and for breakfast they had real bacon and eggs for a change. Not just the gristle and egg powder they ate back in Liverpool.

"Just watch it, Mam, that he does not throw up all over you, he is not used to dipping his soldiers into real egg yolk. It might be too rich for him."

"Don't be silly, you are a growing boy, aren't you?" Annie's mother had no intention to divert her attention away from little David.

"Can I go and play outside, Granny?" Dorothy was getting tired of all the attention showered on David, besides she had spotted some children through the kitchen window, playing hopscotch. A game she was really good at.

"But stay near the front door."

"I will." She ran off before her mam could issue her with more instructions.

"Why did you not tell me about our Paddy?" Annie asked her mother.

"Jesus, Annie, what was I supposed to do, write to you? 'Dear Annie, sorry but Paddy has run off to England, don't know exactly where to and why.' Now you are here, read it yourself."

She crossed over to the mantelpiece without putting David down, took the letter and handed it to Annie.

"You read it while I pour us another cup of tea, your dad should be back from the market soon. You tell me whether it makes any sense to you."

Dear Mam and Dad.

Please do not be mad at me, I am going to England, joining the army. I met this bloke in the pub who is going, and I go with him. I know Dad says the war has bugger all to do with us, but I am still going to do my bit.

PS I'll write to you soon.

Paddy

PPS don't worry.

"What did Dad say?"

"What do you think? He is furious with him. You know he is Irish through and through. If it would not be for you and your sisters over there, he would want nothing to do with the English. And now his only son deserted him too. Annie, can you not find out where he is? Isn't there a central office or something over there?"

"Mam, I don't know, but I'll ask around, I know some of the neighbours' kids have gone to war, maybe their mothers know whom to contact. And there is always William. I know he is in the RAF, but maybe he knows what we should do. Mam, I'll find him, don't worry."

"What time will Flo meet you?"

"They are sending a car to her about eleven. Kieran's family and the other families should already be there. A small boat will be waiting with a representative of the company. Flo was trying to get some flowers. They said we will go about an hour out to sea, but it all depends on the weather. Flo knows that is not the spot where Kieran and his mates were lost, but she is happy they suggested Ballyshannon. It will help his mam and dad as well. We will go to the pub after that. Are you sure you don't mind looking after Dorothy and David?"

Chapter 45

When Annie got back it was early evening and her family was outside in their back garden.

"There you are Annie." Her dad got up and gave her a big hug. Annie immediately worried that something had happened. Her dad very rarely showed his children such emotion, but Annie thought it is best to say nothing and tried to look at her mother who avoided eye contact.

"Come on, sit down. I'll get you some beer, are you hungry? How did it go?" her dad rumbled on.

Now Annie panicked. "Where is Dorothy?"

"Taking her new found friend back to the house next door."

Annie started to relax, maybe she was imagining things. "I think we saw William today."

"William, how could you see William?"

"Well, we did not exactly see him, but when we were out at sea, some planes flew over us. First, we had to all go down to the galley and lay flat on the floor. Flo was on top of her flowers, and you should have seen the state of her when she got back up." A big smile came across Annie's face. "Her carefully styled hair had come undone. Ginger curls hanging down, mixed with yellow petals, smudges on her face." Now Annie burst out laughing. "Sorry, but it was so funny. Anyway, the whole group relaxed after that and what should have been a sombre affair, turned into a right wake." Annie's parents stayed silent and let her continue.

"Mister O'Reilly, the company representative, had brought some whiskey with him. He said in case somebody got seasick, and a sip of that would make them feel better. So we all agreed we felt slightly wobbly, and he opened a couple of bottles. We went about two hours out to sea until we could no longer see any land. I was a bit scared really, but everybody was in such a good mood by then, I did not want to say anything. Kieran's dad kept handing another bottle round, and it was good to see him and Kieran's mam smiling for a change."

Annie took the drink her father offered and continued.

"By the time we stopped, we almost forgot why we were there. But then, everybody did go quiet. Father O'Conner stood up. Read out the names, said some kind words about every one of them, we prayed, and the relatives threw their flowers into the sea. That was when Kieran's mother went to pieces. She shouted his name again and again. Started to sob, of course, and clung on to Flo. Flo did not know what to do. She forgot her own grief for a moment and comforted her mother-in-law the best she could. The boat was really rocking now because the captain had stopped the engine. I was beginning to feel slightly sick, but it was Kieran's mother who threw up. Right on Flo's best shoes." Annie bent over, trying to stop herself laughing, but without success. "I am sorry, Mam, really, but you should have seen it. Kieran would have appreciated today. Just as he would have wanted it."

"What about the planes you saw?"

"Ah, yes, whilst we were all flat on our stomachs in the galley, the captain came down and announced the planes were ours."

"Ours?"

"Well, not ours, ours, Dad. I mean the RAF. First we could not understand why RAF planes were flying right over us, Ireland being neutral and all that. Then he explained there is an agreement with England to let the planes over the Atlantic fly this way. I think he said they call it the 'Donegal Corridor'."

"So you think William was up there, then?"

"We pretended he was, and we jumped up and down, and waved, and hoped they would find and sink the German U-boat that had attacked the ship Kieran was on."

"Mam, you are back." Dorothy came through the kitchen door, holding a glass of milk and sat on the grass next to Annie's mother.

"Granny, what did me mam say?"

"What did I say to what Dorothy?"

Now Dorothy raised her eyes towards her grandmother and then back to her mother.

"Dorothy, wants to stay here with us."

"What are you talking about? Dorothy can't stay here. Her family is back in Liverpool."

"We are her family, too, and if that is what Dorothy wants, you should at least consider it," her father replied.

"Mam, Dad, don't be stupid. Dorothy comes home with me."

"I want to stay here, I love it here, please, Mam, I can go to school here with my new friend next door. She asked me what it is like when the bombs fall. They don't have any bombs here, Mam, and you can play outside all the time. Also, you don't have to take any gas mask with you wherever you go. I could sleep in your room, Mam, and I will write to you all the time. Mam, please let me stay here."

"Dorothy, don't you want to be with you family? What about your dad? Can you imagine what he will say if I get home without you?"

"You could say you evacuated me to Ireland. Yes, that is what you could say, couldn't you, Mam? Surely, me dad would want me safe, wouldn't he? Especially since we lost our Derek already."

Chapter 46

The two friends stood at the railing, watching the ferry dock. David was safely strapped into his pushchair.

"Are you sure you don't want me to stay with you until George is back from work?"

"No, don't worry, I will be alright."

"What will you say?"

Annie shrugged her shoulders. "The truth, that is all I can do."

The ship's whistle blew, and it was time for them to disembark. Flo picked up Annie's suitcase, which seemed to weigh a ton. "Jesus, Annie, what have you got in there?"

"My mam kept most of my clothes, said I didn't need them and filled it with food and treats for the children."

"Not your best dress?"

"Definitely not my best dress. Anyway, when Mam was not looking, I took most of them back."

"Not surprising your case is that heavy, then."

"They are not in there, I know my mother. She would have checked."

"Where are they, then?"

"Our David is doing the ironing job with his bottom." Flo did not get it straight away. "Flo, David is sitting on them."

"Well, you can't take all that stuff with you on your own, I am coming with you, and we will face whatever, together."

"Missus, let me help you with that." A fellow passenger picked up the pushchair with David still inside and carried it down the gangway.

They saw he immediately regretted it when he felt the

weight. "Blimey, young man, what are they feeding you?" He put him down at the docks. Tipped his fingers to his cap in salute and disappeared into the crowd before they could thank him.

George was already at home when Annie accompanied by Flo arrived. It had taken them much longer than they expected. They had missed the tram connection and the next one was cancelled. Nobody bothered to explain why. They heard George's voice coming from the front room as soon as Annie had put the key into the door.

"Who is George talking to? Surely your Peg wouldn't send Grace and Jeffrey back in the hope you would come home today?"

"Sounds like a man's voice, must be a neighbour. George, we are back!"

"Annie, there you are!" Instead of George, a young man in uniform stormed into the hall.

"My God, Paddy, what are you doing here? Do you have any idea how worried our mam and dad are? What the bloody hell do you think you are doing?"

"Annie!"

"Sorry, George, but my mam and dad are going crazy with worry. This one here left without saying goodbye."

"I left a note."

"Oh, you did do that, I must hand it to you."

"Annie, Annie, calm down, come on, take your jacket off. You must be tired. Where is Dorothy?"

At that precise moment, David started to protest by wailing as loud as he could.

"See what you have done." Annie was still facing her brother.

"Annie, where is Dorothy?"

"I better go and change him, and make him something to eat. He only had two bottles of milk since first thing this morning."

"Annie, where is Dorothy? For goodness sake, answer me, woman."

"I'll take him." Flo decided this was a good time to let Annie explain, and she took David from Annie's arm.

"She is still in Ireland," she heard Annie say before she closed the kitchen door behind her and sat David on the lino.

"What do you mean she is still in Ireland? When is she coming home? Is she ill, Annie? Annie, what happened? Tell me."

"George, Dorothy wanted to stay there, that is all. Nothing happened."

"What do you mean, wanted to stay there?"

"George, she wanted to stay in Ireland. Wanted to live with my mam and dad and go to school with her new found friends."

"She can't just stay there."

"Well, she did, George."

Paddy decided he had heard enough, and he was glad that the attention was diverted away from him for the moment. He thought it best to see whether Flo had put the kettle on and went into the kitchen.

"Annie, be reasonable and tell me everything from the beginning and after you have done that, one of us has to go to Ireland and bring her back."

"George, she loved it over there, she is staying in my old room. Mam and Dad will take good care of her. What could I do, drag her back screaming and kicking?"

George was just going to reply, and Annie quickly continued. "My dad says you should think about it before you make a rash decision. She is safe there, and at least one of our children will have a proper childhood without having to dodge the bombs or face food shortages. He said if after a few days you still think it is better for Dorothy to come back, we are supposed to send him a telegram, and he will bring her back himself."

Paddy returned carrying two mugs of tea, handing one to Annie and the other to George. He finished his piece of cake his mother had sent, before he said, "Flo told me you saw the planes flying over."

"What planes?"

"Haven't you heard, the Royal Navy and the RAF sunk that big German battleship, The Bismarck, just off the coast of Ireland last week. Yeah, we showed the buggers."

Ballyshannon, Ireland

"You have a telegram, Missus McGlynn. It's from England."

"Thank you, Aaron."

"Nothing has happened, has it, Missus McGlynn?"

"Just give it to me, Aaron, and thank you."

"We have a telegram, you open it." Annie's mam's hand was shaking when she handed it to her husband who immediately ripped it open.

He looked up and handed it over. "No, just tell me, I don't want to read it. I'll go and pack Dorothy's things, and we have to tell her as soon as she gets in."

"I think you should read it."

Annie's mother took it from his outstretched hand.

PADDY HERE stop ALL IS WELL stop KISS DOROTHY stop LOVE ANNIE stop

Chapter 47

Battleship Bismarck, Atlantic – 27 May 1941

"*Achtung! Achtung!* Incoming enemy aircrafts starboard!"

"We lost the use of the rudder, sir. We lost steerage, sir."

"Reduce the speed to eight knots."

"Sir! Sir! Another hit at portside!"

"Sir, we are taking on too much water, she is listing heavily!"

"Engine room, open the watertight doors and prepare scuttling charges."

"Abandon ship! Crew, abandon ship!"

HMS Dorsetshire

"Hurray! Hurray! We have done it, sir. She is sinking, sir."

"Officer White, prepare to take on survivors."

"Engine Room port twenty-three, reduce speed to five knots, prepare for slow. We are taking on survivors."

"Crew, prepare to take on survivors."

"How many, Officer White."

"110 at the last count, sir."

"Why so few? There were thousands out there."

"We had to abandon rescue. Enemy U-boats alarm, sir."

"Any of you speak English? English, you speak English? E N G L I S H. *Sprechen* English?"

"It's no good. None of them can understand what we say."

"I do, I speak English."

"You, come."

"Sir, this man speaks English, sir."

"What is your name and rank?"

"Egon Schaefer, sir. I am from the medical team. I am a doctor."

"A doctor? No military rank?"

"No, sir."

"Sir, one of the survivors is badly injured. Our medical staff is attending to him, maybe this man could come and help. At least he could speak to him."

"Bring him back to me as soon as he is done."

"Yes, sir."

My dearest Maria,

I have survived. I am a prisoner of war somewhere in the south of England. I have been here for about two months now. We are treated well. Our conditions are very good. Since I am the only one who speaks English, I am the liaison between the German prisoners and the guards. Also, I am the only doctor at the camp. At least it gets me out of kitchen duty. You know me and my cooking skills. I can see your smiling face. Did we have a new baby girl or boy? What did you name our new child? I hope everything is well with you and our friends.

We are allowed to listen to the German broadcast of the BBC every day. I miss you and our children terribly. Please kiss them from me. I will write again soon.

I love you so much,

Yours, Egon

Chapter 48

"When will you be deployed?"

They had gathered in Peg's and Bob's front room. Paddy had stayed with them since the day he arrived at Annie's front door. Peg was glad her brother was living with them, and dreaded the day he would have to leave, and the house would be empty again. She toyed with the idea of asking Annie and George to let both Grace and Jeffrey stay with her during the week. Their new school was nearer to her own than to Annie's, but she knew that would be selfish of her, especially now, with Dorothy living in Ireland and little Derek gone forever. Instead, she insisted that the whole family would meet and eat together most Sundays. It worked well. After the authorities had finally admitted responsibility for the mix up of the evacuation and her children ending up in Freemantle in Australia, nobody dared ask her to hand over any ration coupons or pay for the children's upkeep, as all the other families had to. And now, after they had received the first post, they realised Australia was not that bad after all. Their children sounded so happy, 'although we miss you terrible', they had quickly added. Fancy my children living on a farm, she thought each time she read the letter, which was every night before she went to bed. She pictured them feeding chickens and sheep. Helping in the fields and going to the markets. I must enclose a letter to the nice family who agreed to take them in. It was a funny feeling that total strangers were looking after her children. Watching them grow up, that is what mothers are supposed to do. She should have listened to Annie and should have not agreed to participate in the evacuation scheme. What if they like it so much over there that they do not want to come home afterwards? She had voiced her fears to Annie and Kate, but thought it best not to mention anything to Bob about it. He'd gone really quiet during the last few weeks. Peg worried he still felt that he failed his family. Something he had said when they first found out where their children were. He had spent hour after hour trying to persuade the authorities to let him travel to Australia and bring them back. He knew from the start that this would not be possible.

"But I have to try," he told her each time he came back from a meeting. Peg told her sisters he cried in his sleep.

"Next week. I leave on Tuesday."

"On Tuesday, so soon?"

"Aunty Annie, can we take David to the park?"

When Annie did not answer straight away, Shauna added, "Matthew is getting the dog. Mam, we have to take him for a walk every day, don't we?" She turned towards her mother. "Can we take David with us, Aunty Annie?"

"What do you think, Kate?"

"I think the kids will be alright, Annie, it is only across the road."

"I don't know, George, what do you think? He is still so little."

George cleared his throat and said what everybody had been thinking for a while. "Annie, you have to stop clinging on to David the way you do. He has to learn some independence. He walks, he talks, for goodness sake, woman, let him go with his cousins."

"Where will you go, Paddy?"

"Africa."

"You are going to Africa? Since when do you know that is where you are going?"

"My mate, I came over with, wanted to join the Africa Corps, so I went with him."

"What is the matter with this bloody family? Have we no will of our own? We have not heard from William for a month now, and all because his so-called friend, Joseph, persuaded him to join the RAF. Now Paddy lets his mate talk him into going to Africa. Peg and Bob's kids are in Australia. Dorothy is in Ireland. How much further do we want our family to spread?"

All faces turned towards Kate; they were shocked but not surprised by her outburst.

Grace had taken David from her mother's lap and took him by the hand. She saw the fear in her mother's eyes.

"Come on, Jeffrey, you too. Mam, we all watch him. You want to play outside, don't you, David?"

But David ran back to his mam and put his arms around her legs. "Mam come too, Mam come."

"No, sweetheart, you go and play." Annie freed herself from his hold, kissed him on his head and said, "There you go."

"Look, Kate, we know you are worried about William, we all are. But we are at war, and there is nothing we can do about it." Then Paddy thought about what he had said. "Yes there is, we can fight the bloody Germans, and that is exactly what I intend to do, and if that takes me all the way to Africa, so be it. I am going to do my bit, and I for one hope it was William who bombed the bloody Bismarck."

Chapter 49

Hildesheim, Germany – July 1941

Maria and Hilde cleared away the kitchen dishes after everybody else had left. Hilde had wondered all night why Maria had not been her usual bubbly self, but did not want to press her, trying to find out what was bothering her. Eventually, Hilde could not stand it any longer.

"What is on your mind, Maria?"

"Hilde, can we stay tonight?"

When Hilde did not reply immediately, she quickly added, "The children are already asleep, and it would be a shame to wake them, and walk mine home in the dark."

"I am surprised that after all the years we have known each other, you still think you need to ask me that. You know only too well I would love you to stay, but I am afraid that you think I am taking your life over completely," Hilde replied.

"I got a letter today," Maria said.

"What sort of letter?"

"I don't know."

"What do you mean you don't know?"

"I have not opened it."

"You have not opened it? Who is it from?"

"It is from the War Ministry, it is in my bag. I will get it," she said.

Her hands were shaking when she handed it over. It was a large brown envelope, with an official seal, and it felt that there was something else inside.

"You have to open it, Maria."

"No. I can't. You do it – otherwise I'll just take it home as it is and look at it every day, wondering."

Hilde closed her eyes for a brief moment, trying to gather some strength and took the letter.

Inside was what looked like another letter. She took it out and looked at it. Hilde immediately recognised Egon's handwriting.

"Maria," she whispered, "It is a letter from Egon." Maria did not seem to register what Hilde said. So she repeated, "Maria, it is a letter from Egon."

"A letter from Egon? Are there any other notes with it?"

Hilde turned the large envelope upside down and shook it. "No."

Maria finally took the letter.

"There is some wine left in the kitchen, I will pour us a glass each – meanwhile, please read your letter." With that, Hilde got up and left Maria sitting alone with her thoughts.

Maria was crying when Hilde came back with their drinks. She put the glasses down and rushed over to comfort her friend. "Oh, Maria, I am so sorry."

Maria looked up at Hilde, smiling. "No, no, it is not that, Egon is alive. He is a prisoner of war in England."

"What?"

"Yes, he is a prisoner of war, somewhere in the south of England. Here, read it for yourself."

She wiped her face and nose with her sleeve and then handed the letter back to Hilde.

The greater part of what was written had been blacked out, but yes, he had been taken to England. How and when he did not say. But he was being treated well, and he got the job of looking after the other prisoners' welfare. She was not to worry, he would write again. Maria was ecstatic, the first time in over one year, she was laughing and singing, the two women were so noisy they had neighbours knocking on

156

the door asking whether everything was alright. That night Maria started a diary, just like Hilde's, when Egon came home, he could read all the things his children learned every day whilst he was away. Eventually, Maria said, "England, did you know there were prisoners of war in England?" Hilde looked puzzled. Then it dawned on her.

"The Bismarck. There were survivors from the Bismarck when it was sunk two months ago. Egon did have to report to Hamburg, yes?"

Chapter 50

Garston, Liverpool – December 1941

Annie had not seen Flo at the wash house since the day Flo had started to work at the bottle works. Annie still went there as often as she could afford it, but it was becoming increasingly difficult to have spare money now that she had to pay like everybody else. George had said, "It's a bloody luxury if you ask me." Well, she had not asked him today and manoeuvred the pushchair through the door. She was immediately hit by hot steam and a lot of noise from rattling boilers mixed with chatter and laughter from other women who seemed to be totally invisible inside. Annie shook the water off her coat. It was still pouring with rain outside and she had been in two minds not to come here today, but then, her neighbour downstairs had offered to look after David for the morning if Annie did not mind taking a bit of her washing with her as well. He own husband had an accident at work and was still recovering at home. She had told Annie that he could still not walk by himself, and she felt she did not want to leave him for too long. Two days ago she had asked Annie to come downstairs and sit in her front room whilst she ran a few errands. She had to go and plead with the Corporation to hold the payment for her rent, and she wanted to beg the butcher to give her some bones for a stew. She had whispered this to Annie so that her husband did not hear her. Annie felt guilty taking the money for her washing, but her neighbour insisted, "No, Annie, I am really thankful you are taking my sheets with you. How am I supposed to dry them here without a fire?"

"But you are looking after my David."

"Nonsense, Annie, he is such a good boy, you can leave him here anytime. It gives me something else to do now I can't do my cleaning job. Hope my old man gets better soon, and he can bugger off to work again."

That was why Annie was surprised when Flo appeared just as Annie hung up her washing to dry.

"Flo, what are you doing here?"

"I was looking for you at home. Your neighbour watched me arrive outside and came to tell me where you were. Your David wanted to come with me. Don't look so worried, Annie, she gave him a piece of bread, so he happily stayed with her."

"Don't you have to work today?"

"They gave me some time off."

"What for?"

"To report to the deployment office."

"Flo, have you been drinking? You are not making any sense."

"It's true, Annie, I have been called up."

"Don't be daft, you are a woman."

"Does not seem to make any difference any more."

"Are you kidding me?" Annie looked at her friend with concern. Surely, she was messing her around.

"No, I am not, single women between twenty and thirty are now conscripted."

"Since when?"

"A couple of days ago."

"But you are not single, you are a war widow."

"No, technically, Kieran was a civilian on a Merchant Navy vessel. Annie, I am so scared."

"Oh, Flo." Annie went to hug her friend and held her tight with her wet arms.

"Apparently, I have no family to speak of, no children. They said I looked really strong, and I was an obvious choice."

"No family? Have they gone mad? We are your family, and there is your cousin."

"Annie, I tried everything, believe me. But after the examination, they said they have the ideal position for me. I am to report to the Auxiliary Territorial Services in Rhyl."

"What have you got to do there?"

"That is where they train the women in the anti-aircraft search units."

"Jesus, Flo."

"Even Churchill's own daughter and Princess Elizabeth are helping with the war effort. There are big posters up in the recruitment office. They are supposed to inspire us."

"They have money for printing big posters?"

"Apparently so."

"Let me just pack the washing together, and we'll go home, sit down, have a cup of tea and see whether we can find a reason why you should be exempt."

"I can't, Annie, I came to find you to tell you I am leaving in the morning."

"But it's Christmas next week."

"Do you think Hitler bloody cares?"

Chapter 51

Dear Dorothy,

How are you? When are you coming home? Dad says now the Americans have joined the war, it will be over soon and we can all be together again. He said it was bloody time the Americans made up their mind and came to help us. Please don't tell Gran I used a swear word, but that is what he said. Did you know that Uncle Paddy was here? I had never met him before, but he is really funny and speaks really weird. He used a lot of swearwords when he was here. Does everybody swear over there? You better watch your ~~languge~~ *(how you speak) when you come home. Otherwise, Dad might belt you. He is really getting short tempered these days. Well I am not surprised, even I feel like clouting our Jeffrey sometimes. He can be such a pain. He will do nothing in the house, how he gets away with it, I have no idea. When our Mam asked him to do something, to go and find some coal near the railway line, he always says, yes, in a minute, Mam, I do it in a minute. I just have to finish my homework. You know our Jeffrey, he does not do anything. The other day I felt so sorry for our mam, and Jeffrey being lazy as always, I* ~~snacked~~ *sneaked out without Mam noticing and went to steal some coal myself. I got some, and I was really pleased. I ran all the way home. I fell over, and the coal scattered in front of me. My knees were bleeding. I looked a right mess. But I managed to gather it back up. At home, I put it down in the hall and quickly locked myself into the bathroom because I had torn my dress, and I was all filthy. I heard our mam outside the bathroom door thanking Jeffrey and saying what a good boy he was. I was so cross, I opened the door and stormed passed Mam into the kitchen and went for Jeffrey. I knocked him off the chair, and we both fell down. I sat on his chest and hit him again and again, trying to wipe that smirk of his face. Mam eventually pulled me of him. And guess who got into trouble? Yes, me, of course, not 'wonderful, can't do any wrong', Jeffrey. I am working on something to get my own back, you wait and see. Well, Paddy has gone to Africa, yes, all the way to Africa, but swear you will not say anything to Gran and Granddad, I don't know whether they know where he is.*

Guess what? Our Aunty Flo has been deployed as well. Do you know what that means? It means she also now has to go and help in the war. Our dad says it's a bloody disgrace. Oops, there is that word again. Don't you dare tell on me that I have used the 'B' word. Without Aunty Flo it is really quiet at home, well it would be but for that idiot, Jeffrey. I will ask our mam tomorrow to let me have 2d for the stamp. Do you think there is rationing on stamps? Or can you still just buy them? Well, if I can't get any, I'll have to use a carrier ~~pigoen~~ *pigeon. Maybe old Jack would let me use one from the ones he keeps on the roof at the tenement. So if a bird poops on you and drops a piece of paper, that will be my message to you. Alright? You better write back because I see our mam looking at the postman and he already shakes his head when he spots her waiting at the kitchen window. And you better come home fast because I can't do everything around here, especially with our mam having another baby, and you do remember how ill she was when she had our David.*

Oh, alright, I miss you, my little grotty sister. I wrote this slowly so you can read it.

Love from Grace

Chapter 52

"Where have you been, George? Do you know what time it is?" Annie heard George's key unlocking the door and jumped off the chair, greeting him in the hall.

"Switch the bloody light off. Don't fret, woman, it's those bloody troublemakers, those Chinese." George took his work boots off and walked into the kitchen. "What are you two still doing up?" He asked Grace and Jeffrey. He could just make out their shapes in the flicker of the candle.

"We waited for you, Dad. Mam was so worried."

"Well, since you are still up, you might as well make some tea and get me my dinner, and then put the bath in front of the fire, and fill it with warm water," he continued saying to Grace.

"Actually, Dad, our Jeffrey said as soon as his dad is home he makes him a hot bath, yes, 'that is what I do', he said. He really looked forward to doing this for his dad. You should let him." Grace turned towards her brother with a big grin on her face and hoped he could see it in the dark. She never missed an opportunity to find him some work since the incident with the coal.

"I knew I could rely on you, my son. Get on with it then, and call me when you are done."

Jeffrey got up reluctantly, but could hardly protest that he never said anything like this. He scowled at Grace and was just about to 'accidentally' kick her on her ankle where it hurt most. But Grace had already outsmarted him, and moved behind her dad's chair and put her arms around him.

"Hey, my girl, what is the hug for?"

"I just missed you, Dad."

"What did you mean about the Chinese?" Annie appeared in the doorway with David on her arm."

"Give him to me, woman. You should not carry such a big boy as our David in your condition." David climbed happily on to his dad's lap and took a piece of dry bread off the kitchen table whilst doing so. "I think that bread was meant for me, young man."

"No, David's," he said and showed it to his dad. "I'll cut you another piece." Grace stepped in quickly. She never knew how her dad would react to one of the children taking some food away from him. Sometimes he just laughed, but at other times he would get really angry and even smack them. Her mam said that it is because he works so hard and is really tired after a long day at the docks. Grace had tried to argue with her mam that dad had got angry on a Sunday when she knew full well there was not work that day.

"Yes, Dad, what do you mean about the Chinese?" With Jeffrey busy in the hall trying to heave the bath out of the store, she grabbed the chance to take part in Mam and Dad's conversation without Jeffrey trying to take over all the time. She heard him moaning and groaning at a safe distance.

"They have only gone on strike, haven't they? The whole lot of them. If they think they can come over here and get paid the same as everybody else, they have got another think coming."

"All of them?"

"Yes, the bloody lot. Their union thought they'd make the most of it whilst our boys go and fight a war. There might not be enough workers at the dock, and they can blackmail the government. No bloody chance there, I can tell you. Our foreman says we should send them back where they came from."

"Dad, what will happen to your job?"

"I have to work day and night, that is what, Grace. Go and check how your brother is doing. I am shattered and have to be up really early in the morning. They are bussing some of us from Garston to the Liverpool dockside. Give those to your mother."

"Candles? How did you manage to get those, George?"

"Don't ask, woman. Go to bed. The kids can clean everything away since they are up. Here, take David."

"We got post from Ireland today, Dad."

"Oh, that is good." Grace thought she could make out a happy smile in the dark room.

"Yes, a letter from my mam, and she enclosed a letter from Dorothy for Grace."

"Tell me all about it when I join you in a minute. Now can I have my food and a bath?"

Daer Grace

Thank you for your letter. Is realy great here. I go to scool and play outside. It snowed here ~~yesteryd~~ the other day. I did not tell on you bout Africa and the 'b' word. I ~~wihhsed~~ like to see Anty Flo in her uniform. Write back soon.

Love Dorothy

Chapter 53

Dear Dorothy,

Can you believe it, there is now soap rationing and our Jeffrey is really pleased about it. Now our smelly brother has a real excuse not to have a wash. You should hear him arguing with our mam about it. You would laugh. He actually says he is ~~sacrifizing~~ sacrificing himself so that Dad can use his allocation when he comes home. He did not get away with it the other day. As a special treat, our mam took us to Garston Baths because our dad talked her into us spending Sunday at Aunty Beattie. I think our mam only agreed because we would have fish and chips from Aunty Beattie's fish and chip shop. Dad actually clouted our Jeffrey when he said Aunty Beattie always smelled of fish. I bet you have fish and chips all the time at Gran's. Mam said not to tell you anything about the war, but I heard them talk that there has been a lot of fighting over in Africa, and Dad says we are beating the bloody Germans at their own game. The 'B' word again. I think that means we are winning. Hurray!!!! But don't tell Gran because Mam says they have not heard from Uncle Paddy, and she is worried about him. Have Gran and Granddad heard from him? Write to me quickly if you know so I can tell our mam. Our Jeffrey, he did make me laugh. NEVER tell him I said that. He found an old broom and broke a piece off. He put it over his knee to break it. He cut his skin but could not run to Mam crying. He took Dad's best string and tied the smaller bit to the top. I must hand it to him, it did look a bit like a gun. He puts it up to his shoulder and parades up and down outside the tenement followed by all the other kids and shouts out commands. You should see them. Well at least he leaves me alone most of the day. What he will do when school starts again, I have no idea.

Guess what! Our Aunty Flo came over to see us. She looked so smart in her uniform, and she bought us some sweets. She showed us a picter photo with her and one of those humangous large lights. Almost as big as her. She has to move it around and shine it up to the sky at night to find Hitler planes so that Uncle William can shoot them down. I wished I was old enough to join the war. Then I could wear a uniform just like our aunty. Did you know that Princess Elisabeth is helping in the war? I don't think Princess Margaret is, I think she is too little. Our mam said I should not tell you anything about all of this because over there you are neutuarl I think she meant Irish people don't have to fight. But Uncle Paddy is Irish so why is he fighting? I have to go now. Don't you ever tell on me, alright? Come home soon.

Oh, before I forget we have a new baby brother, Alfie.

Love from your big sister, Grace.

Chapter 54

RAF Martlesham

"Ready, Joseph?"

"Why do we need to take so many?"

"Ours is not to ask the reason why. Joseph, just let's get it over with."

"It's alright for you, you'll be up there again, whilst muggin's here does all the donkey work on the ground."

"Stop whingeing, we have to hurry up."

"These weigh a bloody ton."

"Alright, boys! If you have not loaded every one of them in the next five minutes, we have to leave without them. That would be a real shame. This might be one of our last chances." Wing Commander Brown shouted across from the other side of a Lancaster Bomber.

"Almost done, sir!" William shouted back. The aircraft's noises from the starting engines drowned out most of his reply.

"Hurry, hurry, hurry, we received our orders, let's go."

About a hundred Air Force crew started to dash past Joseph. Joseph sighed, he had volunteered to be part of a Lancaster crew today, but was told he was by now invaluable, manning the radio controls. "Godspeed, William, and come back safely."

"Try not to burn the place down whilst I am gone."

Hildesheim, Germany

Hilde ran. Dragging a screaming Karl-Heinz behind her and pushing Ursula in her pushchair over the cobbled streets, trying not to lose any of the valuable food items she had just managed to haggle for on the black market.

At first, Karl-Heinz had been totally silent, from shock she imagined. How can people do this to their own countrymen? And Karl-Heinz having to witness such horror. What did it say around their necks? Was it only their names? No, now she could see it quite clearly. It was when the woman's body swung around, moved by the wind. 'Hanged for stealing', she thought it had said. The men's bodies were totally still; maybe because of their weight, but they looked so skinny. You could see their ribs. She could have counted them had she remained there. What possessed her to go home via the town square?

"It's fine, Karl-Heinz, we are home in a minute." He looked up at her and immediately fell silent again. Oh, my God. My little boy, how much more can he take? Dear God, make it stop, make it all stop, she thought. Maybe Maria was at home, waiting for her. She did say she was coming over later. After she had been to the hospital. Please be home, Maria.

Karl-Heinz started whimpering quietly. From fear of what he had seen, or because he had soiled his trousers, she did not know. Then she heard it again, the aircraft noises above her head. It became clear to her why she had taken the shortcut over the square. Her brain seemed to replay what the Gestapo and SS had bellowed from some speakers to the crowd gathering around the makeshift gallows.

"This should be an example for you. If you steal from your fellow Germans, you will be severely punished. You all know our Fuehrer will not let his good citizens starve, but even so, these people decided to help themselves to some of your allocated rations. Go home now, and let this be a warning. Heil Hitler."

"Mama, snow." Karl-Heinz pointed towards the sky. The planes flying over had been momentarily blocked out from what did indeed, look like great big snowflakes descending to the ground. Within minutes, Hilde was surrounded by white leaflets, which stretched as far as she could see. Karl-Heinz had left her side and had run through the papers on the ground, kicking them up with his shoes as you do with dry leaves in the autumn. "Mama, look." He picked up an armful of leaflets, throwing them high in the air and stood underneath, watching them fall down on him again.

Hilde bent down to pick one of them up. They did not look the same to her as the, by now, usual propaganda sheets turned out week after week by Goebbels and his propaganda machine. She stared at the paper in her hand until she felt Karl-Heinz moving at her side.

"Mama, what are these?"

"Nothing, sweetheart, somebody must have just lost them." Hilde crunched the leaflet into a ball and put it into her skirt pocket to show to Maria as soon as the two met.

Chapter 55

Garston, Liverpool – February 1944

"Mam! Mam! Look! Come quickly, look!"

"What is it, Grace?" Annie opened her front door. She held baby Alfie in her arms, holding him tightly and feeding him whilst she walked over to where Grace stood outside. She was at the tenement corridor, looking over the wall and pointing downstairs.

"Look, Mam, that soldier coming this way, he looks like Uncle Paddy. See our David and Jeffrey, they are running towards him. Look, he is picking our David up now. Oh, he has spotted us, Mam, it is Uncle Paddy!"

"Uncle Paddy, Uncle Paddy." Grace bent over the wall so she could follow him walking through the door downstairs. Then she thought better of it and turned around and ran down the steps, taking two at a time.

Triumphantly, Grace, Jeffrey and David entered the hall where Annie stood, still in shock, her hands covering her mouth. Finally, she found her voice, rushed forward and flung her arms around her younger brother. "Thank God, Paddy, you are alive." Then she took a step back. "Let's have a good look at you." She pushed him back and walked slowly around him. "Besides being really skinny, all the parts seem to be still there. Oh, Paddy, how I waited for this moment." She hugged him again.

"Mam, shall I make Uncle Paddy a cup of tea, Dad will be home in a minute, Uncle Paddy. Oh, he will be so happy to see you. Mam, do we have enough to eat for Uncle Paddy?"

"He can have my dinner," volunteered Jeffrey.

"Jeffrey, that is awfully nice of you, but they did feed us before we are allowed to come on home leave and see, here, we have extra ration cards to last us all week. But a cup of tea would be most welcome." He smiled at Grace.

"For goodness sake, let the man come in and take his rucksack off and sit down." Nobody had noticed George standing behind them.

"Dad, look, our Uncle Paddy is back all the way from Africa."

"Good to see you in one piece, mate."

"I went past Peg's before I came here, wanted to drop my stuff off. I thought they wouldn't mind me staying with them for a few days. The kids are still in Australia, am I correct?" said Paddy when he eventually sat down after accepting George's best armchair.

"Yes, what did she say?"

"She wasn't there."

"What about our Kate?"

"She wasn't there either."

"Where have they gone?"

"No idea, I thought you might know."

"Maybe both Peg and Bob are working shifts today. Sunday or not, there is a war on and both Fazakerley and Kirby work twenty-four hours," added George.

"But Kate and her kids should be at home."

"Don't fret, Annie, maybe William is at home, and they went out for the day. They are allowed to do that without you worrying about their every move." George happily accepted the bottle of beer, which Jeffrey had borrowed from a neighbour to celebrate his uncle's safe return.

"No, we would know if William is at home, Kate would have sent Shauna or Matthew over for sure."

"Grace, see who is at the door."

"I am busy with Alfie, Jeffrey, you go." Grace still had not forgiven her brother and every job, which needed doing

173

at home, she tried to palm off on him.

He sighed but went to the front door without a word.

"It's Shauna!"

"There you are. I told you William is at home."

"Oh, my God, Shauna, what is it!" Paddy jumped off the chair when a sobbing Shauna stood in the doorway."

"It's, it's."

"Shauna, for goodness sake, speak up."

"There was an accident at Kirby."

"What!"

"What about our Peg?"

"She was working there today."

"Since when does our Peg work in Kirby?"

"Just over a month, Shauna, come on girl, tell us what happened."

"Aunty Annie, I don't know any more, but my mam said to get you and come to our place. She has sent Matthew to Fazakerley to see whether he can find Uncle Bob. One of the neighbours in our street, you know the butcher, he is in the home guard, and he took his van. He is taking Mam and several others out to Kirby right now.

"Don't hang about, come on, let's go." George took charge.

"Wait! George, my mate has a motorcycle. I'll go and get it. We two will go to Kirby. The rest of you go to Kate's as Shauna said."

Annie stood there frozen to the spot.

"Annie, come on. Do as Paddy says, Grace and Jeffrey, get some food from the larder. Make sure you take milk and egg powder for Alfie. Shauna, there is some tea in the pot, have some, it might calm you down." George went into the bedroom whilst he issued the instructions. He had still not changed out of his work clothes.

Chapter 56

ROF Kirby

At first, they couldn't make out anything through the smoke, which greeted them a long way from the actual factory site. They stopped the motorcycle next to a man in home guard uniform.

"Oi, you move on, you can't stop here. And come to think of it, you'd better turn around. You can't get through."

George had already got out of the sidecar, glad for a minute to stand on firm ground. He felt a little queasy. Paddy had been driving like a lunatic. Taking all the corners far too fast for his liking, but not surprisingly, they were looking for his sister after all. So George was not in a mood to argue with this bloke who was so full of self-importance.

"You can bugger off! We are looking for his sister, she was working there today. Come on, Paddy, let's push the bike through the rubble. Don't just gawk at us, give us a hand man, for goodness sake."

"I am not supposed to let anybody go further towards the factory. It is a secure area, you know. See all the fences over there? They are there for a reason. This area is top secret."

Now Paddy had heard enough. He was off the bike and stepping forward he grabbed the guard by the collar and literally lifted him off the ground. George's mouth dropped open, but he quickly recovered.

"This young man has just survived the war in Africa, and you think you can stop him from finding his sister? You pompous twit. Who do you think you are? Come on, Paddy, he is not worth it, let's go."

Paddy let go and the guard dropped to the ground, holding his neck with one hand and reaching for his whistle with his other. Paddy was quicker and snatched it off him, threw it on the ground and stood on it with his heavy boots.

"Don't you dare."

They pushed the bike as far as they could, but then had to leave it behind. They parked it next to a van.

"Look, it's the butcher's van. How did he get as far into the factory grounds?"

"Shauna said he was in the home guard, that explains it."

"Sorry soldier, this is as far as you go." The two were stopped again, but this time by a fellow soldier.

"Mate, my sister was working here today. I have to find out what happened to her."

"I wish I could help you, but I can't let you through. This is a bomb factory, for goodness sake, who knows how many unexploded bombs are under that smouldering rubble over there." He pointed towards the side of the factory, which was no longer burning, but steam and smoke rose into the sky and would be seen for miles.

"Is anybody hurt?" George finally asked the question which had been on his Paddy's mind, all along.

Before they got a reply, Paddy turned to his right. "Look over there. Kate. Kate! Kate!"

He ignored the protest coming from the soldier in charge and rushed over and held her in his arms before she realised who he was. "Paddy, what are you doing here?"

"Looking for you and Peg, of course."

"I am so glad you are here. They have taken some injured women to the hospital. We have to go there and see whether Peg is with them. George, you are here as well, thank God."

"Come on, Kate. I have a motorbike over there. Will you be alright, George?"

"You two go and find Peg at the hospital. I'll see what else I can find out here, and then I'll make my way back."

Chapter 57

"How are you feeling?"

"With everybody making a fuss about me and you having to do our cooking today Annie, good. Yes, I feel good. Help me up."

"I heard that Peg! The doctor said you have got to rest, that was the deal, otherwise, back into hospital," shouted Bob.

"Aunty Peg, can I bring the dog in?"

"NO!" shouted Bob and George together.

"But Aunty Flo has not seen him for ages, and he wants to say hello to Aunty Peg as well. Can I please?" Matthew was not giving up easily.

"For goodness sake, bring him in, but only for a minute. And do not let him jump at your Aunty Peg." Bob relented. "Peg, what are you doing up?" He walked over to where Peg stood supported on her crutches and helped her into the front room. Peg managed to move over to the settee, put her crutches to the side and lowered herself slowly down. "See, no problem. I can do it myself now."

"I'll go and check how Annie and Flo are doing in the kitchen," volunteered George. He thought it was best to let Peg and Bob argue this one out between themselves.

"Peg got up on her own," he said to Annie whilst lifting the lid off a saucepan. "That smells good. What is it again?"

"Irish stew, now get out of the kitchen, George."

"I think I should taste it, maybe you need to add something, like salt?"

"Here, take the spoon, but then out. Ask Grace, Jeffrey

and Shauna to get the plates out. And Grace should cut the bread. But tell her to be extra careful, all the knives were sharpened last week, when old Fred came down the street with the grindstone." All the children in the street loved watching old Fred sharpening knives, scissors and axe blades. As soon as the first child spotted him, the word got round to all the others to run inside and pester mams or dads to let them take the knives and hand over their pennies. Some older kids were allowed to help him. They took the chain off the bike wheel cog and attached it to the grinding wheel drive. This was a really fiddly job, and he was glad the kids were only too keen to do it.

"This was delicious, Annie. You and Flo have obviously not lost your Irish touch. Is there any left?" Paddy, who had been unusually quiet for the last hour, handed his plate over to Shauna who disappeared into the kitchen.

"Are you going back to work at the bomb factory in Kirby?" Flo asked Peg.

"Surely not, you are not going back there are you, Peg? Not after the accident. It is far too dangerous."

"Annie, you are being silly, of course I am going back."

"But Peg, the accident."

"I was nowhere near the accident site, Annie. When we were told to evacuate the factory, I ran like everybody else. Only everybody else was looking where they were going. I, of course, tripped and fell. That is why I broke my leg. And not in the accident at the factory. How often do I have to tell you that?"

"But it is still a dangerous place, isn't it, Bob? Tell her not to go back." Annie now tried to persuade Bob to side with her.

"We need the money," he said.

"Why do you need the money?"

"We are saving."

"What for?"

"For our fare to Australia. There I said it."

"What?" This time it was George who replied first.

"You are going to Australia, when?"

"Uncle Bob, are you going to bring back our cousins?" Shauna carefully carried Paddy's plate with the extra stew and had overheard the last few words.

"Not really, Shauna, we are going to join them."

"WHAT?"

"Peg, what is he talking about, tell me he is only joking, you are not really going to Australia, are you?"

"Annie, come over here and sit with me. Yes, we are going to Australia. We are going to work and live over there as soon as the war has finished." Annie was just going to interrupt when Peg continued, "Let me finish. We got a letter from the family our children stay with. They said there are so many opportunities over there, and Australia needs hardworking honest people to come and live over there. They have a cousin in Canberra who told them as soon as peace has returned there will be a big recruitment drive to get people to come. He said there will be a special fare for the crossing if you are willing to resettle. I think he said it will be ten pounds."

"But there will be plenty of work here after the war, won't there George? You said there would be. Please, Peg, don't go. Why are you even thinking about it? All your family is over here."

"Annie, our children are in Australia."

"Make them come back."

Bob sighed. "Annie, they go to school there, and they made new friends. They flourish, they just love their new life and are looking forward to the day when we can join them."

"Kate, say something." Kate shrugged her shoulders. "I said it all already."

"You knew about this and did not tell me? What about our mam and dad, don't they have a say?"

Bob stood up and walked over to the settee, put his hand on Annie's shoulders and said, "We have made up our mind, nothing will change it. We have already forwarded copies of birth and marriage licences. We want to make sure we do not miss out on this opportunity. Don't make it harder for us than it already is."

"Paddy, what about you, what do you say to all this?"

"I am leaving in the morning."

"WHAT?"

"Sorry, Annie, we didn't know anything about it."

Annie looked at her brother. "Where are you going? No, don't tell me, off to fight this crazy war of yours. A war which is just about tearing our whole family apart."

"Well, I might as well confess, too. I am leaving for London on Tuesday. Apparently the Women's Auxiliary Territorial Services are needed over there," added Flo.

Chapter 58

Dear Dorothy,

Please, please, PLEASE come home and bring Granny and Granddad with you!!!!!!!!!!!!!! When I say don't tell on me this time, I DO want you to tell them what is going on.!!!!!! Make sure you tell Granny! PROMISE!!!!!!!!!! Our mam says our family is ~~disimtigrating disaapering~~ I mean to say that we are losing everybody. Aunty Peg and Uncle Bob are ~~imigrating~~, going to live in Australia. Do you know how far that is? Our dad says it is on the other side of the world!!!!! Fancy that, being on the other side of the world! First our mam thought they were just going to collect our cousins. But NO, they want to live there. Uncle Bob got a letter from the people our cousins live with, and it says there is plenty of work over there and they could have a real good futare. I think that's how you spell it. I don't have time to go to the library to check it out in the dictionary. Anyway, our dad thinks it is very risky going on the word of a total stranger all that way away, but our Aunty Peg and Uncle Bob won't hear a bad word against them, says our mam. Mam says they think total strangers are ~~obvouilsy~~ more important than family.

But this is not all what happened. Uncle Paddy has gone off to fight in the war again and, wait for it, Aunty Flo has moved to London. They need her there she said to work the ~~humangoes~~ enormous lights to find Hitler's planes. All that happened on Sunday. We went over there to cook an Irish stew, yummy yummy! Mam and Aunty Flo did the cooking because Aunty Peg's leg is still in plaster from the accident at the bomb factory. I don't care if Granny did not know about it. You CAN tell her and make sure she is packing straight away to bring you home and talk some sense into our Aunty Peg. Our mam says Granny will be the only one who could do that.

See you soon, little sister.

Love Grace

PS: Our mam does not speak to Aunty Flo any more. She accused her of deserting us. I feel really bad for Aunty Flo, she left the house crying, the war is not her fault, is it?

PPS: I have no time to make this letter more tidy, I wrote it really quickly so you can get it as soon as possible.

Chapter 59

"McGreavy, come with me!"

"With you? Where to sir?"

"There is a war on, McGreavy. Where do you think we are going?"

"But, sir, what about the tower, sir?"

"Not today, McGreavy. The women will have to cope on their own. It's your lucky day, grab your gear. You are with me. You are familiar with the Lancaster I assume?"

"Yes, sir."

"Get the camera, we are taking one along. Go to the wireless position. You have used it in training?"

"Yes, sir!"

"As soon as we are loaded, we are off."

Joseph felt a slap on his shoulder and looked around. "God be with you, Joseph. See you on your safe return." With that, William sped off and boarded a plane further down the line.

"All set, sir."

"What is our destination?"

"52092 N 09571 E."

"Town?"

"Hildesheim."

"Objective?"

"Target built up areas, industries and railway facilities."

"How many on this mission?"

"227 Lancasters, eight Mosquitos in groups of one-eight. Our allies from RAF Croft are joining up with us."

"Ready, sir."

"Roger that."

Joseph had never been in a Lancaster on any of its missions. He had missed his chance to go to 1 LFS Lancaster Finishing School, believing by now, he would never see action again since his spell over in Hong Kong. He could feel the adrenalin pumping through his veins. The sound in his eardrums was overtaken by the noise of the four engines. He rocked back slightly as the aircraft started to move. He regained his balance and adjusted the fit of his headgear and mask. He listened to his own breath for a fraction of a second before he heard the voice of the captain.

"Flight Engineer."

"Ready."

"Navigator."

"Ready."

"Wireless."

"WIRELESS?"

"Oh, yes, ready, sir."

"Bomb aimer."

"In position."

"Mid-upper Gunner."

"In position."

"Rear Gunner."

"In position."

"Tower, Little Audrey is ready for take-off."

"Roger that, Little Audrey. Cleared for take-off."

The aircraft proceeded towards the end of the runway, joining a queue of Lancasters leaving before them. He could spot the Felix, the plane William would be in. Joseph had helped William to paint the black cat on the front of the plane. In his mind, he saw William's writing of the name underneath. Godspeed, William, he thought before his own plane turned to the left, lining up on the runway and gathering speed. He was surprised how bumpy it was, from the tower he had seen the windbag hardly showing any wind at all but still the plane rattled and swayed. It must be the heavy load, he thought, but already he heard the wireless spring to life. He had practised operating the transmitters over and over again. He swung the three large transmitters into position. He knew he had to rely on his wits. He had joined an established crew, wondering what had happened to their previous operator. He knew he had to prove himself to be accepted by them. Joseph glanced briefly out of the window. There must have been about half a dozen other Lancasters on his left. He quickly calculated that if his Lancaster was in the middle position, with three transmitters each, there would be potentially up to nearly forty loud jamming devices. At the worst scenario right now, there would be twenty-one before his unit joined up with the others. Enough to cause some chaos, he smiled to himself.

This must be France, he thought, but before he had the chance to take a better look out of the window to his left, he detected the first blip showing a used frequency. He immediately spot tuned the receiver and listened.

"'*Oh du schoener Westerwald*'," sang a male voice. Yes, right, he knew the Luftwaffe used these codes, wrongly believing the wireless operators would think they had found a German commercial station. He swung the first of the transmitters to the same frequency, pressed the switch, knowing this would leave a powerful jamming warble. Got you, you bastard. The singing voice could no longer be heard. Joseph now brought in the other two transmitters waiting for the next blips.

"Target in sight."

"Roger that."

"Incoming enemy aircraft at nine o'clock."

Joseph felt the plane vibrating from the operation of the front Gunner. The plane turned further left, sliding Joseph momentarily against the window. He quickly straightened himself up and concentrated on his transmitters.

"Got a hit, sir, plane going down."

"Rear Gunner ready for action."

"Roger that."

"We are reaching our target, ready to unload."

"Ready, sir."

"Unload now."

"Bombs away, sir."

Joseph felt the plane lift up. He had heard about this before. He used all his strength not to be thrown off his seat. He glanced out of the window. They were surrounded by a sea of Lancasters. He could not spot any Mosquitos among them. It became increasingly more difficult to see. But he could just make out other bombers dropping their loads. The ground far below the planes seemed to shake. Even from up here, he thought he could feel it. Dark black smoke billowing towards the sky.

"Enemy fighters seven o'clock."

His plane swung round again. He could almost make out the faces of the enemy pilots, but then the plane turned away from him and concentrated on a Lancaster coming directly towards them.

"McGreavy, the camera, take photo evidence." He heard the pilot's instructions and tried to feel below him for the camera without taking his eyes off the enemy still to his left.

"They got a hit, sir, a hit on one of ours."

"Front Gunner into position."

He felt the vibrations again; his hands were shaking while trying to put the camera against the window. He could see a plane spiralling down to the ground. As it took another turn, he clicked, then realised what he had just seen. A black cat.

"The Felix, sir, they hit the Felix!"

"William!" was the last thing he remembered.

Chapter 60

Hildesheim, Germany – 22 March 1945, 14.00 hours

"Run, run, faster, faster."

Hilde was the first one to hear it. A roaring sound behind them. She looked around and then up. The sky, which a moment ago was blue and bright, was now dark and threatening, like a flock of angry birds looking for their prey.

The noise was deafening. There, again and again, getting closer and closer. They grabbed the hands of their children. Maria pulled the pushchair with her right hand and held Manfred with her left. He stumbled and fell to the ground. She lifted him back up and half-running, half being dragged along, they carried on. Nobody made a sound.

Hilde had a tight grip on Karl-Heinz and Ursula on her arm. Her weight slowed her down, but she ignored the ache in her muscles and the pain from the scratches on her body. The undergrowth was dense, the brambles tore at their dresses. A noise right in front of them. They froze. A young deer stopped in its tracks, looked at them and sped away. A whistle sound, reminding them of fireworks, at New Year's Eve many years ago, right overhead. Followed by a split second of silence. Total silence. Then an ear-splitting sound and the earth moved around them.

"Down! Get down."

They all fell to the ground. Hilde tried to shield Ursula and Karl-Heinz with her body, and covered her head with her arms. Like a hailstorm, debris of stones, splintered wood and soil were hitting their bodies.

"Hilde, are you alright?" Maria was up first, brushing dirt off her clothes.

"We have to leave the pushchair. Hurry, hurry."

They kept running, ducking in and out of trees, feeling the soft moss under their feet. Hilde stopped, and looked around to take a deep breath, and to make sure that they were alone when they got there.

The place they were running to, Hilde knew it well. They should be safe there. She saw it only a few metres away. "Hurry, hurry."

The door, although it was old and the hinges were rusty, was still strong. There was a big iron ring on one of the sides, you had to pull hard and hold it with both hands to lift it up. "Quick, quick in here." She ushered everybody down the stairs, took a large stone, which lay in the shadows and used it to hold the door up slightly. She could not know how long they would have to hide here and would need the air. They crouched down and huddled together, the floor in their hiding place shook, the walls vibrated, and dust was sprinkling down on them. They had reached the place just in time.

Hilde blamed herself that they were here in the first place. Maria had her doubts that they should take the children for a day in the woods, but Hilde had been very persuasive. After all, there had been no bombing for a few weeks, and it was such a beautiful day today, she had argued with Maria.

"Mama, I am scared." Hilde pulled Karl-Heinz closer to her and held him tight. Ursula had her small arms around her mother's neck, not wanting to let her go. "Bang, bang," she said.

They took comfort by sitting closely together. It was dark, but they were starting to adjust. The light, which was coming from upstairs through the gap was unusually dim for this time of the day. It was only around 2pm in the afternoon. Why did it look so dark?

They smelled smoke, which seemed to be creeping down through the space at the top and was now rolling down the stairs to get them.

Then another sound, silence and an almighty blast, they fell backwards from the impact. Hilde heard a rattle from the door above me, dropped Karl-Heinz on the floor and raced upstairs. She reached the door just before the stone rolled away. She used her back to lift it up with all the strength left inside her.

"Maria take the children, I am going to have a look."

"But we have not heard the all clear."

Seventy-five, seventy-six, seventy-seven the stones steps were steep and slightly damp, and she had never climbed them this fast. There were only twenty steps to go. Those were the round iron staircase, which was narrow and could be slippery at times. It was best to hold on to the rail. The paint was flaking off, leaving sharp edges, cutting her hand as she continued upstairs. Reaching the top, she wiped her hands on her dress, leaving dark smudges.

Hilde had reached the top of the tower. She knew it would be deserted now, and it was quite safe to come here again.

Just in case, she crouched down, slowly lifting her head above the last step and looked around before she stood up.

She saw the smoke rising above the town. Smoke which must be at least 500 metres high, she estimated. It made her choke, and she felt slightly dizzy. She lifted her dress to cover her nose and mouth whilst trying to feel her way towards the front of the tower, edging forward very slowly. Last time she was here, she had seen that part of the walls were crumbling and some of the stones had fallen down to the ground below.

Through the smoke, she could make out fires in the distance, but could not see clearly, and there was nothing she could do from here. They had to get back.

Hilde carried Ursula on her hip and held Karl-Heinz with a firm grip with her right hand. Maria and Manfred were behind her. They made their way to the edge of the forest. The journey back was blocked by fallen trees, smouldering rubble, and there were fires burning to their left. It was easier for Hilde to climb over the fallen trees first. Maria lifted the children over one by one, and then Hilde helped Maria. After the third climb, they were getting into a routine and managed to go faster. They reached the end of the woods, there they stopped dead trying to take in what they saw. Waterloo Street, which should have been in front of them, had disappeared. Where there once were houses, there were now smouldering ruins. Fires burning everywhere. People shouting, running. Trying to save their homes by forming lines, passing buckets of water to each other. Children were wandering aimlessly, lost, crying, looking bewildered, some sitting on the remains of walls, which a short while ago had been their home. The way back was like running the gauntlet, they weaved through the chaos around them, fell over but got up and continued on. They passed bodies in the streets, people searching to identify members of their families, calling out names of loved ones. They tried to shield the children from what they witnessed. Maria took Ursula for a while. They kept urging the children to go faster. Children who had lost the will to walk.

They saw some of their furniture on the pavement, long before they got to the apartment. Frau Bucker spotted them and came running, shouting all the way.

"Hilde, Hilde, come, come!!"

Frau Bucker's voice was lost in the noise. Hilde saw the

roof of their apartment block was burning. Flames shot up into the sky.

"Hilde, the school, leave everything and get to the school!"

All blood drained from Hilde as she said it. The children. They had sent the elder children to school in the morning.

She looked down at her feet, her stockings were torn, bloody scratches across her legs, a heel on one of her shoes was missing. She snapped off the other and ran.

Chapter 61

RAF Martlesham – Friday 23 March 1945

"Sir, permission to go on leave, sir."

"Reason, McGreavy?"

"Permission to travel to Liverpool to visit William's family, sir."

Wing Commander Brown was quiet for a few moments, then said, "Do you think it is a good idea? They will have already received notification."

"It's my duty to speak to them, sir."

"Alright, permission granted, you are on compassionate leave. Here, take it to the office and get your ration cards and travel warrant. Report back a week tomorrow."

"Thank you, sir." Joseph packed his bag and asked whether he could get transport to the nearest station. Nobody argued with him on this occasion. Something they would always do when asked to use a jeep and a driver for their private journeys. A group of Air Force men went to see him off, including the crew from Little Audrey. The plane Joseph had been on when he witnessed his friend being shot down. Like everybody, Joseph was aware of the big casualties and losses the RAF bombers conceded after every mission. But this time, it happened to their very own men.

"You did good, McGreavy." His pilot came over to him and shook his hand, followed by the navigator, engineer and bomber crew. He knew he should be pleased he was accepted by them as their new wireless operator.

The journey from Martlesham to Garston, Liverpool took many hours. There was no direct route, and Joseph changed trains three times before he got to Lime Street Station. But to him, it seemed far too quick, and in no time, he reached Kate and William's street.

Throughout the journey he had tried to work out what he would say, or what kind of reception he would get. Maybe Kate and the children were not in at all. What would he do then? Knock on Peg's door?

But Shauna, Matthew and their dog were outside in the street, although it was getting dark. They spotted him as soon as he turned the corner and ran towards him.

"Uncle Joseph, do you have any news about our dad?" Shauna shouted before she reached him.

Joseph shook his head.

"Is your mam in?"

"Yes, and Aunty Peg and Uncle Bob. I think Aunty Annie is coming over later," volunteered Shauna.

Joseph bent down to stroke the dog, which rewarded him by licking his hand. At least he welcomes me today, and I don't even know his name, he thought.

"I never asked, what did you call your dog?"

"Felix."

"Felix, but that is a name for a cat, surely."

"Yes, but is our dad's favourite name, and he wanted me to be named Felix, but our mam did not let him. So Shauna and I thought if we name the dog Felix, our dad will let us keep him," said Matthew, smiling from the memory when they presented the puppy to their dad.

Joseph's knock was answered by Bob, and it took Bob a while to collect his thoughts.

"I don't know, Joseph, whether it is a good time."

"Who is it?" called Kate.

"It's Joseph."

Kate came flying towards the front door. Then stood perfectly still before her hand reached up, and she slapped Joseph across the face.

"It's your fault, everything is your fault. If you had not persuaded him to go with you to enlist, my William would be still alive. Now get out of my sight!"

Peg had appeared behind Kate and tried to pull her back inside.

Joseph had not moved and just before the door slammed in his face, he had time to reach out and stop it from closing. He followed Kate inside.

"Kate, I can't be one hundred per cent sure, but I think I saw some crew parachuting from the plane. I saw the parachutes open, just before the plane hit the ground."

Chapter 62

Garston, Liverpool – 8 May 1945

"Mam, we need red, white and blue. Look, come and look, everybody is wearing some." Grace took her mam by the hand and dragged her through the front door on to the corridor outside and pointed down. "See, everybody." She looked at her mam's face and corrected herself. "Well almost everybody. Please, Mam, have another look. We must have something."

"Alright I'll have another look, take Alfie for a moment."

"Mam, can I have something red, white and blue as well?" David stood on tiptoes in order to see better over the wall. "Grace, you can bring my dress-up clothes downstairs. I'll go and help my mates," he added.

"What?"

"PLEEAAASSSE, Gracie."

"You always call me Gracie when you want something, David." But she smiled at him. She found it increasingly difficult to refuse when he looked at her with his pleading dark brown eyes. Sometimes he reminded her of a little deer, caught in the headlights of a car, that look of his.

"I'll come with you, David, and don't bother bringing me anything down, Grace, I am not wearing any bloody red, white and blue," said Jeffrey.

"Lucky for you our mam did not hear you."

"Well, dressing up is for girls or little boys," he quickly added. "Myself, I'll go to the Co-op and give Dad a hand with carrying the beer." Maybe he'll let me have a drink today, he thought, after all, it has been declared a public holiday. In any case, if he doesn't, me and my mates have already figured out how to lift a bottle or two without being noticed.

A week earlier, George had run most of the way home from his night shift at Garston docks. He was shouting to people on the way. People shouted back and waved at him. When he reached the tenements, he went to every door in their block, waking everybody up, shouting and laughing. Annie heard the commotion from her kitchen and quickly opened the door. There stood George, sweat dripping from his forehead, several of their neighbours behind him, most of them still in their nightclothes.

"George, for goodness sake, what is going on?"

"The point is, my dear Annie, nothing is going on, that's just it, nothing."

"George, you are not making any sense, what happened?"

"That bloody Hitler is dead, that's what's happened."

Grace was wearing her mother's best white printed skirt, which she had rolled up so it would not reach the ground. Her mam gave her one of her dad's blue work shirts. Surely, he would not mind today of all days, and a red belt was tight around her waist. She had tied her long hair and put a white scarf around it, with a knot in the front. Not bad, she thought when she walked past the mirror. Alright, normally I would not be seen dead like that, but who cares today? After all, we are celebrating. She hoped none of the boys she had started to hang out with after school, together with her best friend Jo, would see her. Not that they would mind. But they would tease for sure. No, her greatest concern was that her mam, or God forbid, her dad found out she had a boyfriend. Paul and she had kissed for the first time last week. They had fixed a date to go to the cinema together. God only knows how I will be able to get away from home for that. It's about time that Dorothy made an appearance.

After all Grace was leaving school for good next month and had found work at the match works. Grace held Alfie by the hand and slowly helped him to walk down the staircase. Her mam had tied a red and white tea cloth around his neck. It was hanging down, and he looked a little bit like a knight, but he was happy. It was too long of course, and Grace had to make sure he did not trip over and fall. He could make quite a racket when he hurt himself.

"Gracie, Gracie, over here, what did you bring me?" David waved from the other side of a long row of tables, which were set up in the middle of the tenement blocks.

"You are getting far too cheeky for my liking." She laughed when she fought her way to where he stood. "Here, sort it out yourself." She threw a bundle of clothes towards him and all of his friends dived on it.

"Oi, me mam gave it, so I have the first pick."

"And me mam baked some scones, so I am second," Freddy quickly added, pushing the others aside.

David lifted some of the items his sister had brought down. And then looked around to see what the other boys were wearing. Hadn't his brother said, 'dressing up is for little boys?' He did not feel little now being nearly six years already. No, dressing up was no longer for him.

"Hurry up, David," Freddy edged him on.

"I tell you what, Freddy, you being my best mate, and your mam baked those scones, you go first."

"Really?"

"Yes, really, let me just take the cowboy hat and cap gun." David left the rest of them fighting over the booty whilst he set off to help with the bunting. All of their neighbours seemed to own some or even a flag. Either an English white and red, or the blue/white/red Union Jack. If he played his part helping to put things up, maybe nobody would realise one or two had gone missing. Mister Cain from number 4a had a Box Brownie. He trusted David to guard it for a moment. He had forgotten to put a film in and was rushing back to find one upstairs.

"What you got?"

Freddy found his way over to David, looking more like a pirate, little to do with wearing the right colours, but grinning from ear to ear. "Here."

"One of your mam's scones?"

"No, we don't need to pinch those, there are plenty of them and are me mam's."

"A sausage roll?"

"David, come over here with the camera, we want to take a picture of everybody in our block together."

"I'll save you a place next to me, hurry up." Freddy went back to his mam who turned round and beckoned David to come over.

"Where is your mam?" George put the bottles of beer at the end of the first table, helped by Jeffrey, who was looking for a chance to disappear amongst their neighbours unnoticed.

"Mam is taking the cake out of the oven, she'll be here in a second," replied Grace, who saw David helping Mr Cain setting up the chairs.

"Come on, everybody, photo time. You too, Missus Jones. Leave your window open so we can hear the radio."

"Here it comes. Everybody quiet."

God Bless you all. This is your victory! It is the victory of the cause of freedom in every land. In all our long history, we have never seen a greater day than this. Everyone, man or woman, has done their best. Everyone has tried. Neither the long years, nor the dangers, nor the fierce attacks of our enemy have in any way weakened the independent resolve of the British nation. God bless you all.

"Hip, hip, hurray! Hip, hip, hurray!"

Chapter 63

Hildesheim, Germany – 8 May 1945

Hilde and her friends were sitting in front of the radio.

Winston Churchill, the British prime minister, had just spoken, proclaiming victory and the end of the war in Europe. They had waited for some sort of formal announcement most of the day. Maria did her best to translate as quickly as possible for the others to understand.

Their town, Hildesheim, had already been taken over by British and American forces over a week ago. From the reaction on the soldiers' faces when they arrived, they realised how shocked they were at what they found. That the town they were supposed to be assigned to was reduced to rubble.

The first thing the soldiers did was to set up tents near the airfield about two or three kilometres north of the street Hilde lived in. When the wind came from the north, they could smell the cooking from the camp. More and more people, mainly young women and boys started to wait outside their camp in the hope of a hot meal or the odd piece of chocolate.

With the arrival of the British and American army came the disappearance of the SS and Gestapo men. Not one of them was anywhere to be seen. It was like the earth had swallowed them up.

"I have heard that most of them are burning their uniforms at night in the cellars of bombed-out buildings. If they spot anybody coming to check what the fires are about, they scatter or claim ignorance. If questioned, they deny ever having belonged to the party," Frau Bucker told everybody when they gathered in the kitchen, peeling potatoes and cleaning vegetables for the stew they were preparing. No bones to make the stock today. The butcher did not want to part with any just for a set of silver cutlery. He was holding on to whatever he had left for a higher bid. They hoped the soup would be some nourishment for the twenty people they wanted to cook for.

Hilde and her friends never knew that they had a prisoner of war camp in Hildesheim, but apparently there had been one nearby. This was the first building to be liberated by the British troops. After that, they took over most of the garrisons still standing. People who had made their homes there after the last bombing raid had to move on into overcrowded schools, the cinema, theatre or any houses, which were judged to be big enough to accommodate more people. Some people moved out altogether in the faint hope of finding accommodation in nearby villages.

In the garrison, at the end of Hilde's street, although now British, they were allowed to keep a small partitioned-off corner and continue the efforts, with food collection, distribution and a soup kitchen.

"You have been looking out of the window for a long time now, Hilde. What are you looking for?" Frau Bucker asked.

Hilde turned around to face her, wiping her wet hands on a tea towel.

"My Karl, I am hoping to spot Karl when he comes round the corner. I want it to be me, the first person he sees when he returns."

Chapter 64

Garston, Liverpool

Flo sneaked up behind David and quickly put her hands across his eyes. "Guess who?"

"Aunty Flo! You are back. Did you bring me anything?"

"There is nothing like little boys making you feel welcome, is there?"

David gave her a puzzled look.

"Come here you, the first thing I need is a great big hug." David happily obliged, after all, she did not say there was no treat.

Flo reached into her bag.

"Sherbet, my favourite, how did you know?"

"Say I just guessed." Flo looked further down the street and then asked, "Where are the others?"

"Our Grace is now working at the match works, and Jeffrey, he is always somewhere where he shouldn't be. That's what our dad says."

"Your mam and Alfie?"

"Upstairs, making dinner."

"David!"

"I am here, Mam!"

"Come upstairs and look after Alfie." Annie leaned over the corridor wall and spotted Flo.

"Flo!"

Flo, with David by her side, was greeted at the front door by a waiting Annie, who rushed towards her and put her arms around her friend. "Oh, Flo, it is so good to see you. When did you get back?"

"Last night, back at being a civilian."

"What is a civilian, Aunty Flo?"

"David go and play with Alfie."

"But, Mam!"

"No, 'but Mam' about it, and look at you." Annie looked David up and down. "You are filthy and how did you tear your shirt, and why do you have those scratches on your legs? Have you been playing at the waste ground again? How often do I have to tell you not to play there? Go and wash your hands."

"But, Mam."

"David, don't let me tell you again."

David knew better, when his mam reached this stage, it was always better to do as he was told.

"George kept an eye on your house as promised, was it alright when you got there?"

"Everything was fine. Thanks again. I went past the bottle works to see whether I could get my old job back."

"And did you?"

"Of course not. All the jobs are already taken by all the other women coming from service. We were the last to be discharged."

"I'm sorry, what are you going to do?"

"I'm quite cheesed off about it, I can tell you, so much for going to serve your country. After that, you are on your own."

"What about the wash house?"

"I hoped to get better work than that but I'll go there and ask. Better than nothing I suppose. Now tell me everything that happened whilst I was away."

Flo pulled a kitchen chair, sat down and picked up the mug of tea Annie had put there.

"William is still lost, for one thing."

"What do you mean lost? When? How? Annie why didn't you let me know?"

"It was all too distressing, I'm sorry, Flo. I really am."

"So, tell me now."

"Mam, Alfie is taking my book."

"For goodness sake, David, give it to him, he is only little."

"But, Mam, it's my best Rupert annual. He will ruin it."

"David, if you do not give it to him this minute, I will give it to him myself."

David got off the floor where he was sitting, and pulled one end of the book to prise it out of Alfie's hands. With a final pull, he freed it from his brother. Immediately, Alfie started wailing.

"Mam, I am giving it to him, in a minute."

"David, don't make me send you to bed without anything to eat." David wiped the book clean with his sleeve. Took a deep breath, sighed and started to tear the book in half, right in the middle. It took all his strength, but he succeeded. He held each part in one of his hands. Looked at it a final time and looked down at the floor where Alfie was sitting holding up his hands. "There you are Alfie, you can have it now."

"What are you doing, David?"

"Nothing, Mam, I gave Alfie my book." David came over and stood behind Flo, out of his mother's reach.

"Tell me, Annie. Tell me everything about everybody from the very beginning."

"David, be a good boy, here are the ration coupons. Go to the Co-op. We need extra potatoes and bacon. On this occasion, you are allowed to lie a little."

"What, Mam, what am I allowed to say?" David temporarily forgot about his Rupert book.

"Tell him your relations have just returned from abroad, after a long time, fighting that Hitler. And don't take no for an answer. Tell him we need it 'on tick'."

"He'll never remember all that!"

"You will be surprised how resourceful our David has become. Yes, he will get the words all wrong, but he will bring back what I asked for. You wait and see."

Flo almost spilled her tea; her hand was shaking from laughing.

"Oh, Annie, it's so good to have a laugh again. But now really, tell me what happened."

"Well, William got shot down over Germany shortly before the end of the war. Must have been one of the last bombing raids they had to do, I think. Anyway, Joseph was in a plane next to him and saw it all happen."

"Jesus." Flo had put her tea down and put her hand over her mouth, worried she might scream the words out loud. "How did Kate and the children take it?"

"Well, when Joseph turned up at their front door, I think she was ready to kill him. She is still blaming him because William joined up. Bob said she actually slapped him across the face."

"No!"

"Yes, but he just stood there and took it. Then he followed her in and said that he thought he saw the crew bailing out. He saw parachutes opening before the plane went down."

"No!"

"Yes. Now here is where it gets complicated." Annie heard Alfie wailing from the front room. "Alfie, come to your mam," she shouted.

A sobbing Alfie walked into the kitchen, one side of the book in each hand.

"Alfie! What did you do? Our David will go mad!"

Alfie only wailed louder. "Hello, Alfie, see what your Aunty Flo has for you. A sweetie."

He calmed down immediately and climbed on Flo's lap.

"Now where was I?"

"At the stage where it becomes complicated."

"Ah, yes, well. Now England and their allies occupy Germany, right? And the town where William is lost is where the British are. Joseph has volunteered to be stationed there. He is determined to find William, one way or the other. I think he is either there already, or he is just about going there."

"Blimey!"

"We don't know any more right now."

"What else is happening?" Paddy got back a few weeks ago. Still in one piece, thank God."

"That is great, where had he been?"

"You know he has gone really quiet. He has not said anything yet. He was here for a very short time."

"Has he gone back to Ireland?"

"No, he will never go back. He found himself lodgings in Liverpool."

"What is he going to do?"

"George told him there would be work for him at Garston docks, but he was going to have none of it. Said he needed to be on his own for a while. He is working at the docks but in Liverpool."

"Well it least he is close by, that is great."

"And..."

"And what?"

"Dorothy is coming home next week. My mam and dad are bringing her over."

Annie could no longer hide her smile; she was beaming.

"Oh, Annie, that is wonderful news. It is so good to have everybody back, isn't it?"

Chapter 65

Hildesheim, Germany – October 1945

"Karl, Karl!" Hilde shouted his name over and over again. She had spotted more returning soldiers coming down the street. They had to pass by her kitchen window on the way to the garrison where they were required to hand in any remaining weapons and be listed as having returned from war.

Hilde had no time to check on her new baby, but grabbed Ursula by the arm and pulled her outside, running as fast as they could towards the soldiers before they disappeared from her view. This time there were about thirty of them. Maybe one of them was her Karl.

"Karl, Karl?" A wounded soldier, his head heavily bandaged, one leg shorter than the other, supporting himself on wooden crutches looked at her. She hoped for a sign of recognition. He raised his head, which until then, had been bent down towards the ground, looked at her and shook it.

"Do you know my Karl?" she asked another.

"Where do you come from?"

The next, "Are you all from the same brigade?"

"Do you know whether there are more soldiers on the way?" Hilde asked the same questions day in and day out. Always being greeted with the same sad looks.

"Karl, Karl." Maybe he was at the back of the group.

Frau Bucker came to find her and took Ursula, ready to carry her back. Only now did Hilde realise Ursula was still in her pink pyjamas and bare feet.

Maria, who was now living back in her old apartment,

had seen the soldiers returning before they entered the street where Hilde lived and had reached Hilde the same time as Frau Bucker. Maria and Frau Bucker looked at each other.

"Karl, Karl." Hilde would not stop shouting his name.

"Hilde, we have to go inside now." Maria took her gently by the arm, trying to guide her back.

"But I have to find my Karl, maybe these soldiers know where he is and when he is coming home," Hilde protested.

"I will ask my husband and his comrades whether they have met others on the way. What is your husband's name and which brigade did he serve in?" A kind woman came over to where they stood. Hilde had not noticed before that most of the soldiers were accompanied by women and children, all beaming with happiness and hanging on to their husbands and fathers.

"It's alright, Hilde, you go in with Frau Bucker. I will pass all the details on," Maria volunteered. Once back inside the apartment, Hilde for the first time in weeks noticed what state her kitchen was in. Ursula was standing on a dirty floor, a piece of bread in her hand and her face and fingers covered with homemade jam. Unwashed dishes in the sink, potato peel on the floor beneath the table, dirty nappies in a bucket, which should have been in the bathroom. The surface of the kitchen table was covered with everything that would normally be stored carefully in the larder. Maria entered and stood behind her.

"How long has my kitchen been like that?" Hilde asked nobody in particular.

"It has been going on since you gave birth to your baby, almost three weeks ago. Frau Bucker and I, we have coped as well as we could. Most of the time I still sleep here to keep an eye on things."

"Three weeks, I've had my baby for three weeks?"

"Yes, and you have not even named her yet. Time is running out, and you have to register her birth soon. We have spoken to the doctor who has notified the Town Hall Birth Registrar, but you have to go there next week."

"But how can I do it without Karl?"

"Hilde, what would Karl think if he saw you and your home in such a state?" Frau Bucker spoke firmly.

"Where are my other children?" Hilde was surrounded by a fog that was slowly lifting.

"Klaus and Renate are at school and Karl-Heinz is in the kindergarten, I took them there this morning," Maria told her.

"What does the rest of my apartment look like?"

But before anybody answered, Hilde heard her baby crying, turned on her heels and went into the bedroom. There she was, in her cot, her dummy lying next to her, her little hands balled into fists, as if in protest at being ignored by her mother. Hilde picked her up, sat on the bed and cradled her in her arms. She opened her blouse and started to feed her. The infant looked at her, as if she had never seen her before.

"It's alright, Erika, Mama is here," Hilde said and then she heard the bedroom door close softly behind her.

Chapter 66

Garston, Liverpool – December 1945

"I don't think this is right, George, they fought with us, side by side, to beat that bloody Hitler and now we do this."

"Nowt to do with me, Bob."

"Yes, but what do the others think?"

"What others?"

"The dock workers."

"They think what most of the people in Liverpool think, they are Aliens and we need the jobs for our own people. Tell you what, Bob, their problem is having gone on strike when they did. That alienated a lot of good people, that did."

"But what choice did they have, they had to do what the unions told them to. You know how this works."

Bob got up to get the newspaper from the little table at the side.

"Here, I'll read you this."

J.R.Garstang, the Immigration Officer in Liverpool, protested strongly to the government, without success. This was backed up by the Chief Constable of Birkenhead, who pointed out, in letter after letter, that contrary to the statement by the authorities that:

"Listen to this, George."

The Government called them: An undesirable element of Liverpool.

"What do you say to that, George? An undesirable element of Liverpool they say. Anyway, let's continue."

> The Chief Constable of Birkenhead spoke in support of the Chinese workers pointing out the law abiding nature of the Chinese.

"I don't know, Bob, law abiding, he said?"
"Yes, and there is more:"

> The compulsory repatriation of Chinese seamen from Liverpool has already begun with several hundred leaving this week. We interviewed the first seamen to leave and some of them were not reluctant to go because of the hostility towards them during recent years. Others were totally devastated.

> We spoke to Mister Lee Kee Lo, who begged us to tell his wife and children what had happened. He went out to do the shopping ten days ago and was apprehended with several others whilst out. He was taken to the Immigration Centre without being allowed to contact his family. "My wife thinks I have deserted them. Please go and visit her. Tell her I love her and I will write soon. Please," he pleaded with the reporter.

"I don't know, Bob, it's not what I hear at the docks."
"Wait, I have not finished."

> Inside information from the council has come to our attention. Although some of the deportations are up to their discretion and Chinese dock workers with an English wife and children can apply to have their cases heard. However, this is being totally ignored for the reason that we ourselves require the houses they now occupy due

to the heavy damage to buildings sustained during the bombing raids.

"You look quite pale, Bob, are you alright?"

Bob had bent over and put his fist on to his chest. That seemed to ease the pain a little. The sharp stabbing pain he felt occurred more frequently these days, and the intervals between them got less and less. He had not said anything to Peg about it, and he put off seeing the doctor until the medical was over for his emigration papers to Australia.

Chapter 67

Germany – January 1946

Joseph swung the large duffle bag over his left shoulder. He slipped and the weight of it almost made him fall backwards on to the snowy ground. Only the strong hands of a fellow RAF Corporal holding on to him managed to save him from embarrassment. Blimey, how did Kieran carry this around with him, he thought. "Mind how you go, McGreavy."

"Thanks, mate."

"Where are you posted to?"

"Hildesheim."

"Me, too. Where do you report to?"

"Lederbur Kaserne, and you?"

"Same here. Any idea where it is?"

"Not the foggiest."

"Well let's find out when we get there."

"Yes, alright."

"I heard Hildesheim was heavily bombed. Were you part of the crews?"

"Yes."

"Did you see a lot of action during the war?"

"No, that was the only time. And you?"

"None at all. Mind you, I wanted to. What was it like?"

"My best friend got shot down, and I watched it happen."

"Jesus, McGreavy. Is that why you want to go back?"

"Yes, I am going to find him and bring him home, but whatever you do, don't tell anybody that's why I volunteered."

"No sweat, mind if I hang around with you, maybe I can be useful?"

"I would like that."

"Great, let's get to Hildesheim and find that Lederbur Kaserne of theirs."

"You two, over here, the bus will take you to the station. Show me your papers."

Joseph put the duffle bag back on to the ground and felt in his uniform pockets for his papers. He knew exactly where they were; he must have checked his pockets at least a dozen times since he set off from Liverpool.

"Good, when you get there, report to the guard at the gate. Here, you need this as well – it shows them you have been cleared to go. Once there, you will be assigned to your quarters. You two travelling together?"

"Yes, sir!" they replied in unison.

"Here, give me that."

"No!" Joseph quickly bent down and retrieved the duffle bag. Annie had trusted him with it when she gave it to him. Flo would not mind, she had said, but he had to promise to bring it back and he was not going to let it out of his sight.

"It's bloody freezing, another thing they forgot to tell us. By the way, I am Rick." He blew on his hands and reached out to Joseph. He took it and replied. "I am Joseph, come on let's go, it must be warmer in there."

They found two seats together at the back of the green military bus and put their gear on the spare seat in front of them. When the bus reached the main road out of the airport, it slowed down and then stopped. As far as they could see, were snow-covered ruins. Women and children tried to remove the snow off the road so the bus could get through. It seemed a hopeless task, no sooner was one stretch cleared, then fresh snow had fallen on to the ground. Young boys wearing only sweaters and trousers, their hair covered in snow, had run beside their bus, some using their fists to bang on the doors.

Joseph got up from his seat and went to the front to speak to the driver, "What do the children want?"

"They hope you have something for them to eat, even a piece of chocolate."

"I have some rations in my bag, can we stop and give it to them?

"We are not supposed to, but we are almost standing still anyway, get your things and I'll open the door."

"Rick, what have you got in there?"

"I still have my chocolate and biscuits, that's all."

"Give it to me."

"What about you and you?"

Several of their comrades searched their bags and gave Joseph what they could spare.

"You can open the door now."

The driver got out of his seat and turned the handle and opened the door. Joseph climbed out, careful not to drop anything.

The boys just stood there silently, watching and waiting. Joseph saw immediately, he did not have enough for all of them and sighed. He pointed to the first two boys and beckoned them to come forward. He gave a small packet of biscuits to the taller one and said, "You, you," pointing to both of them. They nodded and left the line. The next two boys stepped forward, and he repeated the process until all the children had something to share. He went back to the bus and started to climb in. The first boy came back tapped him on the shoulder and said, "Danke."

Nobody spoke for the rest of the journey. At the train station in Hanover, Joseph and Rick had to fight their way through the large crowds trying to work out where to go from there. One of the platforms, which looked like the only one that was not damaged, had a train waiting. They found a soldier in British uniform.

"We need to get to Hildesheim."

"Find some room on the train and get out at the first stop."

Their journey took less than an hour, and they were standing all the way. A woman and her daughter got up to make room for them, but they both had declined. From where they stood, they were able to take in their surroundings. All the voices around them were in English. None of the German passengers seemed to speak and avoided eye contact with them. An army officer entered the carriage from a connecting door and stopped at the first passenger.

"Papers." Shaking hands fumbled in pockets and produced what looked to Joseph like some kind of identity card. To them the officer only nodded.

Joseph was relieved when the train stopped and they could leave.

Joseph and Rick were the only two who got out and stepped into a foot of snow. No snow had been swept away here. It kept falling down heavier now through the damaged station roof.

"Come on, let's go, Joseph, it will be getting dark soon. Who knows how far this Kaserne is? What's it called again?"

"Ledebur."

Outside the station, they looked in horror at what greeted them.

"Christ, Joseph, I thought Hanover was bad."

Not one of the buildings around them was still intact. Snow and ice covered bomb sites; big craters were in the road in front of them. Women and children rummaged in the ruins looking for something useful or maybe for old possessions. To the left of them, a line of women cleared a site, taking brick by brick and removing the ice and mortar with small hammers. Other women and children stacked them up on the roadside. Army vehicles tried to manoeuvre around them.

Joseph stopped an old man who was just about to pass him.

"Lededur Kaserne?"

The man did not seem to hear him and was walking on. Joseph went after him and held him back by his heavy overcoat. The man spun round and lifted his fur hat, which until now had covered most of his head. "*Wie bitte?*"

"Ledebur Kaserne," repeated Joseph, this time louder.

The man pointed ahead of them and carried on.

Joseph and Rick walked in the direction the man had pointed. At the next crossing, Joseph approached a woman carrying a heavy basket. As soon as she saw them approaching, she covered the contents with a cloth and spun round to walk in the opposite direction. But she was too slow.

"Ledebur Kaserne?" he asked again. The woman looked like she tried to figure out what he said and then her face lit up.

"English?"

They nodded.

"*Einumer strasse da, see?*"

They could just make out the street name and nodded.

"*Links, verstehen?*"

She pointed to the left. Joseph and Rick nodded. She counted on her hand and continued, "*Zehn strassen, rechts. Verstehen.*"

Joseph worked out by the numbers she held up and the way her arm pointed, she meant ten streets turn right.

"Thank you," he said.

"How long?" added Rick.

He received a blank look. He pointed to his watch.

Again she used her hands and indicated fifteen minutes.

"Thank you," said Rick and was just about to leave.

"Don't mention it," she replied in perfect English.

"What?"

"I am Maria, I am going that way, so you can walk with me."

She smiled and stretched out her hand to greet them.

Chapter 68

Garston, Liverpool

"But, Mam, these are girls' shoes."

"David, try them on, if they fit we'll take them. Who would notice?"

"Look, they don't fit, look, Mam, they are too big."

"Your dad will put a bit of old newspaper in the front."

"I am not wearing them, and that is it. I'll wear my old ones."

"How much?"

"Tuppence."

"I'll take them."

David bent down to retrieve his old shoes.

"Mine, give me." Alfie had sat on the stone floor in the church hall, and he now grabbed them, stood up and ran off."

"Oi, come back you. Give me my shoes." But Alfie had already disappeared between the other mothers rummaging around the donated clothes.

"Mam, can I have these long trousers? Most boys have started wearing them, I am freezing, Mam."

"No, these are far too big, and there is nothing wrong with your old ones. Don't even think about it, David, you tear the ones you're wearing, and your dad will give you a good hiding. We don't have money to burn, you know, and I need some clothes for Dorothy. She has outgrown everything from Grace already."

"She should have stayed in Ireland."

David just managed to duck out of his mother's way, the

new shoes still on his feet. He had spotted Freddy, his mate.

"Nice shoes!"

Freddy noticed David's face. "Look, they are not that bad, if we rub the shiny leather with some stones and mud, they'll look worn, and nobody will notice." David did not look that convinced and Freddy continued, "Let's get out of here before our mothers find something else. Look at this cardigan my mam got me. I will forget to bring it home the first day back from school. I'd rather freeze to death."

"Come on, David."

"Race you."

They were out of the door and round the corner before their mothers could notice. Freddy stopped and was trying to catch his breath. "Don't think you can run in those shoes."

"Yes, I can!" David sped past his mate and reached the waste ground first. He hurried up the hill and looked back to see whether Freddy was following him. He had not noticed the pile of bricks in front of him, tripped and fell over and landed on top of the rubble.

"Blimey, David, are you hurt?" Freddy had caught up.

David sat up and looked at the damage.

"I am not crying."

"It's not that bad, hardly any blood, looks more like scratches, your mam won't notice."

"My mam will think I did it on purpose. I've torn my trousers, and she'll tell my dad about it."

"No, she won't. Come on, let's look for treasure."

"Where was your David off to in such a hurry?"

"Our David? He is..." Annie looked around, still thinking David was standing next to her.

"He just scooted out with his mate, Freddy."

"I don't know, those two, I am glad every time they come home in one piece, I can tell you, Flo." Flo put Alfie back on the ground. "And this one, I just caught him in time before he could run after them. Anyway, your David won't get far without shoes. Come on Alfie, give your mam David's shoes."

"Mine," he said and pulled them towards his chest and folded his arms around them in case his Aunty Flo was going to try and take them away.

"Yes, they are his now, David just got some new ones. Anyway, I thought you were working all day on Saturdays?"

"Not a lot on at the wash house, but I have to go back soon to switch the boilers off and lock up. I was working on my own today. I just wanted to see you."

"That's lovely, you have not been round the last couple of weeks, and I was starting to get worried. Look, they have a tea urn over there – let's sit down."

One of Annie's neighbours gave them both a cup of tea and a homemade biscuit. Alfie got a glass with squash.

"What do I owe you?"

"It's free, Annie, Father O'Brian must be feeling especially generous today, or he hopes we'll turn up at church this Sunday. Here take another biscuit, whilst nobody is looking."

Annie put her bag on the floor and Alfie climbed on her lap, keeping a watchful eye on Flo. He wanted the biscuit and his squash very badly, but that meant letting go of the shoes. He resolved the matter by trusting his mam to look after them, carefully placing them on top of his mam's bag. He could watch them from where he sat. He kept looking between them and Flo whilst his mam let him have a drink. He almost forgot to eat his biscuit.

"How is Dorothy getting on now, has she settled back in alright?"

"No, it's a real worry. I should have never let her stay in Ireland with my parents."

"Don't be daft, Annie, what about all the families who

evacuated their children. You did the right thing. You wait and see."

"Well, I bought her a few things today. Hope that will cheer her up a little. She is growing so fast, Flo."

"Have Peg and Bob had any more news about Australia?"

"Yes everything seems to be going smoothly. They are waiting for their final paperwork and a date when they can leave." Annie took another sip of tea. "Peg is getting so excited. She has started packing, and she asked me what I wanted her to leave behind."

"Like what?"

"Like in the house."

"What do you mean?"

Annie could not contain herself any longer. Her face was beaming.

"Well, Flo, if you would have been round more, you would have known that Peg and Bob have put us down to get their house in Stamfordham Drive."

"You are kidding."

"No, honest, but we have not told the children, just in case."

"Annie, I am so happy for you. That makes what I wanted to tell you less painful."

Annie's face fell. "What do you mean?"

"I am going back to Ireland."

"No, please Flo, please, don't go back. I need you, I can't lose you again."

Flo put her hand on Annie's. "Annie, I am not going to go back forever. I promise you. I'll be back. I just need to go home for a while."

Chapter 69

Hildesheim, Germany

"Joseph, I thought you were supposed to look for your mate, William, and not at every pretty German woman we pass?"

"You heard the same as me, right? There are still several airmen unaccounted for, and not all the remains of the planes have been located."

"Well, at least you got the official nod that you can look for him as long as it does not interfere with what you have been assigned to do, and it does not interfere with their investigation. Those were their precise words, right?"

"Yes, and I have come up with a plan."

"You have got a plan?"

"Yes, Rick, I do."

"And that would be what?"

"I think you and me should start speaking to the people who were actually here when he went down."

"Who?"

"The locals."

"By that you mean the women."

"Right!"

"Now that is a plan I like, there is only a small problem. We don't speak German."

"I have thought about this, too."

"You have?"

"We have a free weekend coming up, right? So instead of having a few beers, we go out there and become the helpful occupier. After all, we freed them from the Nazi regime, so they should be grateful. With me so far?"

"Not exactly."

"Remember the woman who showed us the way when we arrived."

"How could I forget her? Maria?"

"Yes, she went into a house not far from here, so we are going to hang around that area until we spot her. Her English was not bad. We start there. What do you think?"

"I think you have a plan, McGreavy."

"Have you seen that English soldier outside, Hilde?"

"What soldier?"

"The one across the road, see over there, he is lighting a cigarette. He has been here before, he keeps looking at you."

Hilde walked over and stood next to Maria, who had moved the curtain for a better view.

"No, Maria, he is looking at you."

"Hilde, go and ask him for a cigarette."

"Maria, we don't smoke."

"He does not know that."

"But I don't speak English."

"You can say 'cigarette, please', can't you?"

"Of course. But why?"

"Hilde, I know it's hard, but we are running out of supplies and have very little left we can trade with. We can get butter for a few cigarettes. Plus, despite your old clothes, you look lovely, please go and ask him."

Hilde glanced out of the kitchen window to make sure he was still there but could not spot him. "He is gone, Maria, just as well. We are not that desperate that we have to beg the English for help, surely, Maria."

"We are, Hilde, and he is standing right under the window, I can smell his smoke."

Hilde stopped what she was doing and took her apron off. She straightened her dress with her damp hands and walked over into the hall. She heard Erika moving in her cot beside her bed and went into check that she was still asleep. Erika had moved her blanket. Hilde put it back, hoping she would sleep a little longer. She glanced at a reflection in the mirror and stopped. Her hair looked out of place. She picked up the comb from the dressing table, took a couple of hairpins from the drawer and pinned it back. Not bad, she thought. If I tighten the belt a little more, nobody would notice my bony body underneath the flower print.

"Aunty Maria says you are wasting time, Mama." Ursula had followed her to where she stood.

"Shh. Don't wake Erika. Tell Aunty Maria I am going," Hilde whispered.

I hope he is gone, this is not right, were Hilde's thoughts as she opened the apartment door and stepped into the hallway. One flight of steps and she would be through the door to the outside.

"Have you gone yet?"

Hilde sighed, Maria was right, but pride made her hesitate again as she reached for the door handle. Too late. The soldier outside had seen her. He was at the door in two fast strides and held it open.

"*Guten tag.* My name is Joseph." He held his outstretched hand towards her.

"Me, Hilde. *Haben sie eine Zigarette fuer mich?*"

"Cigarette?"

"*Ja, bitte.*"

Joseph took the packet from his uniform pocket. "Here, take it."

"No, *eine.*"

"Take the whole packet."

"No, *danke.*"

"Yes, please," said Maria who appeared behind her and snatched it from Hilde's hand. "I thought I recognised you," she said to Joseph.

"You know him?"

"Yes, Hilde, he is one of the soldiers I told you about."

"We are in the Air Force, actually."

"All right, Joseph from the Air Force, why don't you come inside."

"Mama, what does the soldier want?" Ursula was standing at the apartment door.

"Nothing, sweetheart."

"But why is he here, Mama?"

"I didn't know you lived here," Joseph said following Maria up the stairs.

"I don't."

"But I thought...?"

"No, my friend, Hilde, lives here."

"Where do you live?"

"Why do you want to know?"

"No reason."

"Joseph, I think you'd better go, it's a funny coincidence you turning up here, don't you think?"

"It's no coincidence, Maria, I was looking for you."

Maria stopped in her tracks and pulled him back by his sleeve just as he was entering the hall. "Why were you looking for me?"

"Maria, calm down, I am searching for my mate, and I hoped you could help. That is the truth."

"You'd better sit down and tell us everything from the very beginning."

Maria noticed Hilde putting the kettle on and quickly shook her head. Hilde put the kettle back and sat down, lifting Ursula on her knee and hoping she would find out soon what was going on. Ursula put her mouth to her mother's ear, placed one hand over it slightly and whispered, "What is Aunty Maria saying?"

"We would make you a cup of tea, we know how much you English like your tea, but we don't have any," Maria continued.

Joseph lit another cigarette and offered one to Maria and Hilde.

He looked at Hilde. "Your daughter?" Hilde just looked at him.

"Yes, Joseph, that is obviously her daughter, another one is in a cot in the bedroom, three more at school with my two. Now you know everything there is to know about us, but we know nothing about you. Is Joseph even your real name?"

"Yes, of course, Joseph McGreavy."

Joseph then took a deep breath and told Maria about their original mission, his friend being shot down and that he had heard nothing from him since then. He spoke to Maria, but his eyes were focused on Hilde.

Maria was quiet for several minutes when Joseph stopped talking. Eventually, she said, "After you leave, I will tell Hilde everything you have said. Have you any idea what a difficult position you put us in? The only reason, I really mean the only reason, I have not yet asked you to leave is, my husband, Egon, is a prisoner of war in England. Somewhere at the south coast of England. In every letter I got, he told me how well they were treated, and I know my husband well enough to know he told me the truth. This is why I will try and persuade Hilde we are going to help you to find out what happened to your friend."

"Your husband is a prisoner of war in England?"

"Yes."

"How come?"

"He was on the Bismarck when your lot had nothing better to do than to sink it."

"I am really sorry, Maria."

"Joseph, it's not your fault, any of it, and come to think of it, it's not our fault either. Maybe a bit of good comes of it, what do you say?"

"Why has your husband not been released yet?"

"Look, don't worry about that right now, I have been notified that he will be released with the first prisoners returning."

"How will you be able to help me?"

"Egon was a doctor at the hospital here. I am going to ask around."

Chapter 70

At lunchtime the next day, Klaus opened the front door. Hilde was in the bedroom changing Erika's nappy.

"Mama, there are two soldiers outside."

"What sort of soldiers? And where do you mean?"

"English and at the front door."

"What! Don't let them in, Klaus. Close the front door. Two, you said?"

Yes, Mama, what do they want?"

"Tell them to wait."

"But they don't understand me."

"Klaus, that is their problem. Go and close the front door and tell them to wait."

Klaus looked confused, but did what his mother told him.

"*Warten sie bitte,*" he said and closed the door in front of them.

After a few minutes, Hilde appeared, holding Erika on her arm. Klaus had put his jacket on and went past Hilde out of the door.

"Hilde, this is Rick, I hope you don't mind that I brought him along."

Rick took his field cap off his head. "I hope we are not disturbing you, but Joseph said I could come as well."

"*Klaus holt* Maria. *Warten sie bitte,*" said Hilde, pointing to the staircase, indicating that they should sit there and wait.

"Wow, I wouldn't like to be on her wrong side," whispered Rick after Hilde went back inside.

"Yes, isn't she great?" replied Joseph. Hilde could hear

Maria's heavy breathing before Klaus pressed the doorbell. She hoped Maria would listen to her and have a check-up at the hospital next time she went. Maybe she could persuade her to do this the same day as she was going to make enquiries about Joseph's missing friend.

"Hold on, I'll just ask Hilde whether you can come in," Maria told the two still sitting on the steps as they'd been instructed by Hilde. "What do they want, Maria? We only met Joseph yesterday. Are you sure he is telling the truth?"

"I think he is, Hilde, I phoned a nurse I know yesterday. I did not give her the whole story, but I did not need to. She will make a few discreet enquiries tomorrow and will ring me back."

"You think she will find something out?"

"No, I don't, but she will give me any information she has and most likely can tell me what I can do next. Let's wait. Shall we let the two in now and see what they want?"

"Yes, ask them to come in."

Joseph put his duffle bag on to the kitchen floor and took the seat Hilde pointed to. Rick stood next to Maria, close to the window.

"Klaus, take the toy cars into the sitting room. You can all play there."

"Your children?" Joseph had not taken his eyes off Hilde.

"*Ja,* Klaus, Renate, Karl-Heinz, Ursula *und* Erika, *mine.* Hugo *und* Manfred, Maria's."

Joseph nodded, and Hilde felt proud she had been understood.

Renate, still hiding behind her mother, started to lose interest and being allowed to play in the sitting room was too tempting.

"Come on, Ursula, let's go."

Joseph stopped them in their tracks. "Wait, I have something for you."

Renate did not understand what he was saying but stopped anyway.

Joseph bent down, opened his duffle bag and got out several small bars of chocolate. One by one, he handed it to the children and was thanked politely. Renate ask her Aunty Maria how to say *'danke'* in English. Karl-Heinz had waited. Joseph stood up to hand him some chocolate and Karl-Heinz said, *"Ich will ihre schokolade nicht. Und sie sollen gehen."* He then turned to Hilde and continued, "Mama, these are soldiers, why do you let soldiers into our home? Tell them to go." Hilde's heart missed a beat. She knew it would take a long time until Karl-Heinz would forget all the horrors he witnessed during the war. If ever, she thought.

Hilde crouched down, so she could be the same height as her son.

"Karl-Heinz, it is alright, I know they look like soldiers, but they are not real soldiers, you see. These people are here to help us to rebuild our town. You know, like the playground you used to go to."

Karl-Heinz did not look that convinced. Hilde stood up and went behind him, turned Karl-Heinz around so that he would face Joseph and asked, "Joseph, haben sie Kinder?"

Maria, who had stood very still during the Karl-Heinz outburst quickly translated.

"Yes." He touched his jacket pocket and Karl-Heinz took a step backwards, almost standing on his mother's feet.

But Hilde held her ground.

Joseph took two small photographs, which he had kept with his ID papers and stretched out his hand towards Karl-Heinz.

"Shall we ask him the names of his children?" Karl-Heinz looked up at his mother and nodded. "Go and ask him."

He walked towards Joseph and said, *"Wie heissen*

deine Kinder." Joseph said a silent prayer, hoping he had understood correctly.

"Girl Sheila, boy Ken." He handed the small photos to Karl-Heinz. Hilde could see a little girl with blonde curls and a small boy with dark hair. Karl-Heinz studied them for a minute and then handed them back.

"No, for you," said Joseph, putting them back into Karl-Heinz's hand and closing his fingers around them. The photos stayed where Joseph had placed them and Joseph held the chocolate out again. This time Karl-Heinz took it and wordlessly walked away, followed by his mother.

"Oh, boy," said Rick. "Where is his father?"

"Karl was killed on the Russian Front."

"Jesus, Joseph, let's go."

Joseph stood up just as Hilde came back into the kitchen. He reached into his duffle bag and removed the items and placed them on the kitchen table. More chocolate, two tins of biscuits, a tin of coffee, a bag of tea, flour, cocoa, three tins of milk, sugar and a piece of bacon wrapped in some paper.

"Thank you for trying to help us. We know how difficult this is for you. We'd better go now. If I can have a piece of paper, I'll write my information down. If you find out anything at all, would you mind leaving a message at the gate? The guards will pass it on."

"Ask him whether next time they come when they are off duty, could they wear civilian clothes?" Maria translated what Hilde had said and Joseph nodded.

"When can you come again?"

"In three days' time."

"That is good, I might know by then. Can you come in the morning? The children will be at school."

Chapter 71

Garston, Liverpool

"David, open the door, somebody is knocking."

"Where is Dorothy?"

"Never mind where is Dorothy, just see who it is."

"But I am playing with Alfie."

"David!"

"Alright, I am going."

"I come."

"Mam, our Alfie wants to come."

"David, for goodness sake. It's just the front door. Go and open it."

He got up and went the short distance through the hall. Outside on the walkway, he couldn't see anybody. He walked over to the wall and looked down, then ran inside to his mam.

"It was Aunty Peg and Aunty Kate."

"Where are they then?"

"They are just walking away, down the road."

Annie stood there dumfounded. "David if you are not downstairs in a second to bring them back, I will smack you myself and not wait until your dad is home."

David did not like the sound of that. His mam had never threatened to punish him herself, so this must be serious, he reckoned.

"Auntie Peg, Aunty Kate, wait, wait."

"Why are you in your socks, David?"

"Me mam sent me to get you."

"We thought maybe she was not yet back from work. We were just going to wait in the park."

"She is home now."

"Let's walk back then."

"I think I'll stay outside."

"In your socks?"

"It's not that cold, I'll take them off."

"David, I don't know what is going on, but you are not staying outside like this."

Peg took his hand and started to pull him behind her.

"Aunty Peg, I am coming, you don't need to take me by the hand." David scanned around hoping none of the other boys had seen him being held like a little kid.

"I have put the kettle on," shouted Annie from the kitchen when she heard the front door open.

"What brings you two here all the way to Garston on a Wednesday?" continued Annie, still having her back towards her sisters. "Wait, have you any news about..." She had turned around looking from one to the other.

"No, no news about William, if that's what you mean."

"I can see from your faces something is up. David, go and play outside with Alfie."

"Told you I'd stay outside, Aunty Peg."

"Let me get the cups, Annie." Kate walked past Annie towards the kitchen cupboard and Peg pulled herself a kitchen chair and sat down.

"How is that job of yours?" Kate carried on.

"Out with it, I know something is up."

Annie put the teapot on the table, holding the handle with a tea cloth. Last week, she had burned her hand, and it was still sore from all the chemicals she used to clean the floor at the Co-op. She did not want to tell them about it. She was grateful she had got her old job back. George seemed to be working fewer hours every week. He said last night he might have to find another job.

"Bob has to go into hospital."

"He has to go into hospital? What for?"

"He needs an operation."

"He needs a what?" Annie put her teacup back before she had the chance to take a sip. She would have choked, otherwise.

"It could be serious. Annie, I am so scared." Annie reached over the kitchen table and took both of Peg's hands.

"Peg, take a deep breath, we have always been here for each other. Now tell me everything."

Kate shot a quick glance over to Annie, who got the message that this was not good.

"Bob kept having these pains. I had noticed him grimacing sometimes and bending over. But when he noticed that I had watched him, he quickly straightened up and told me onions gave him wind. The other week, he came home late from work, made some excuses about it – I don't remember exactly what he said. But he had secretly seen the doctor."

Peg paused and had a drink before continuing.

"He had to go for some blood tests and X-rays, so he had to tell me. Telling me all the time there was really nothing wrong with him. He got his results last week. He has got cancer."

"Oh no! Where?"

"In his lungs."

"Oh, my God, Peg, he will be alright, won't he?"

"The doctor said to be optimistic. But he also said Bob should have seen him sooner."

"Why didn't he, Peg?"

Peg took a deep breath. "He did not want the Australians to know about it. He wanted all the paperwork in his hands."

"What does the Australian Office say now?"

"We are not going to tell them, Annie."

"You're not?"

"No, Bob might be totally alright after the operation. We are just making some excuses that we have to delay our departure, that's all."

Chapter 72

Hildesheim, Germany

Maria put the phone down. That had been quite a lengthy conversation with the nurse from the hospital. Several times, Maria had to ask her to repeat what she had said. Maria wondered whether it was really a bad line or the nurse had whispered every word. She would have not been surprised if it was the latter. People still thought they could not speak freely. She was told that there had never been any English airmen at the hospital during the war, and none were admitted afterwards. She checked all the records as far as she could during the last few days, hoping nobody would ask her what she was doing. When she was leaving to go home the night before, Sister Theresa stopped her. The Mother Superior wanted to have a word. The nurse was worried she would be dismissed for what she had done. To check through admission papers and records would not be easy to explain. I should have never agreed to do this, the nurse said at least four times during her conversation with Maria. Maria felt she had no choice but to remind her that it was Maria's husband, Egon, who had saved her brother's life despite having been told there was no hope. The nurse spoke more clearly after that. Maria was supposed to come to the convent, which was attached to the hospital, on Friday, after morning prayers. Mother Superior would be expecting her.

All this sounded quite promising, and she told Joseph when they met again at Hilde's that she would go there and report back to them the following weekend. Despite

Maria's original misgivings about it, she was becoming intrigued.

"Maybe we can find something out about Joseph's friend, William, after all," she said to Hilde, holding on to the pram with Erika whilst Hilde put the shopping bag with potatoes, carrots and onions over the pram handle.

"Have you told your sister about this?" she then asked Hilde.

"No, they are still in Lueneburg, at Erich's parents', and are not due back for several days."

"Did they find an apartment here in Hildesheim?"

"Yes, in the Goebenstrasse. They can move in at the end of the month. And Erich found work."

"That is good news. What is he going to do?"

"He is going to work with the railway company. I think my sister said something about becoming a train driver."

"I like your sister. I am glad they will live here."

"Do you want me to come with you on Friday?"

"I don't think there is any point. I bet Mother Superior only sees me because Egon was a doctor at their hospital. Anyway, if we can get some of those free bones from the butcher today, and I still have some dried peas, you could make us a great big pot of stew, and we can all eat together like we used to."

"Why is it always you, Maria, who has the best ideas?"

"Maria, how are you? Please take a seat."

Maria had arrived early at the convent. She had to wait for about one hour before she was taken to meet Mother Superior. She did not mind waiting. It was so peaceful inside the inner hall. Maria had wondered whether it was always like that, even during the war. How many people had taken refuge here? Were they allowed to stay, or did nuns have to follow instructions and hand them over to the authorities? As soon as Maria laid eyes on Mother Superior, she had her answer. No way would this nun make a pact with the devil.

"Thank you for seeing me, Mother Superior."

"Have you got any news from your husband?"

"Yes, Mother Superior. He is well and should be released soon."

"I heard he was taken as a prisoner of war to England, is that right?"

"Yes, Mother Superior, and he has been treated well."

"I am glad to hear that. He is welcome to continue to work here at the hospital as soon as he feels well enough. You tell him that, Maria."

"Thank you, Mother Superior, I'll let him know. He will be very grateful."

"Nonsense. Maria, he is one of the best doctors we ever had. Now tell me all about this English man you are looking for and why."

Maria had given a great deal of thought to how much and what she would say to the Mother Superior. However, when she sat in front of her and looked into her piercing eyes, only the truth would do. When Maria stopped talking, she sighed and sat back. Mother Superior had held the small wooden cross hanging from a long chain around her neck in her hand whilst Maria spoke. She now folded her hands in prayer and placed them on the table in front of her.

"I appreciate that you have been so honest with me, Maria. I have decided to tell you what I know. I had heard about the English plane being shot down and some of the airmen taking to their parachutes. I do not know what happened to them exactly, but the Sisters of Kloster Marienrode will be able to tell you more. I will write a letter to them this afternoon, advising them to expect you. Don't worry, Maria, you will be welcome there. Leave it a few days. I have already prepared a note for you to take along."

Mother Superior got up from her chair and walked over to a small desk underneath the window. The window overlooked the courtyard Maria had walked through earlier. She opened the desk drawer and handed Maria a white envelope with the convent's crest. She smiled at Maria and said, "God be with you, Maria."

Chapter 73

Hildesheim, Germany

"Has Joseph been over?"

Maria and Hilde were going to help clear some of the rubble from outside of the Saint Elisabeth Church, in the *Moltkestrasse*. Normally, they would stay nearer to home. There were many bomb sites to clear in their own neighbourhood. However, behind the church, the former church hall housed several families whose homes were completely destroyed. The Red Cross ambulance could not get through a few days ago, and one of the residents had died because of it. So the local vicar spread the word, and Maria, Hilde and several of their neighbours were going to help today. Most of the other churches in town were too damaged to be used at all. Although the Saint Elisabeth Church was Catholic, the priest there and the vicar from the Saint Jacobi Church in the town centre held their services there on alternative Sundays. Maria had long stopped worrying about religion.

"Joseph? No, I have not seen him."

"What is that box then on the kitchen table with your name on?"

"That was in front of my door when I came back from the kindergarten. I waited for you to open it."

"Let's see what we have got."

"I want you to take it, Maria."

"Me, why?"

"You also have a family to feed and you do all the running around for Joseph. I think this is yours."

"Let's not argue about it, you do most of the cooking, remember?"

Hilde took a kitchen knife from the drawer and handed it to Maria to use it to cut the string, which was securely tied around the brown box. "No, let's not cut it, it looks really useful. I'll try and untie it. We have a minute, don't we?"

"Yes, we have agreed to be there in half an hour. The vicar knows Ursula has started to go to the kindergarten, and I had to drop her off first."

"Didn't he find the place for her?"

"Yes, and she loves it there."

"At least we know the kids have milk and a slice of bread while they are out most of the day."

"Klaus came home all excited yesterday. Instead of just a chunk of bread, they had dripping on it. You should have heard him talking about it. If it had not been really funny, I would have cried."

Hilde dressed her little girl who had been playing quietly on the kitchen floor with one of Klaus's cars. "Braunschweig is not in the Russian zone, is it?"

"No, it's on this side, otherwise we'd have no chance of getting there. Not even the RAF could arrange that."

"I still can't believe that my sister, Erika, is the only one from my entire family who managed to flee here to us in the English occupied zone. Everybody else is exactly where they didn't want to be."

"Maybe they can come here as well, they have your address, don't they?"

"I worry that it is too late for that, Maria. Isn't that what Joseph told you, no movements are allowed into different zones."

"Yes, he did."

"I still can't believe what you found out at the convent in Marienrode."

"Me neither. I did not even think I would be allowed in that day. But Joseph could only get the vehicle that morning. Mind you, I made him drop me off well before we got there, and I walked the rest of the way. If anybody had seen me arriving in an English military vehicle, I would never have stood a chance. As it so happens, Sister Francisca saw me immediately. I had actually hoped to be able to have a look around first. I did see some bomb damage on the left side and nuns were doing some sort of work there. I saw others in the inside garden tending some vegetable beds. I did get some curious looks. Maybe I should have dressed down a bit for the occasion."

"I didn't know you had clothes to dress down?" interrupted Hilde, smiling at her friend.

"Well, I don't. Anyway, I handed her the note from Mother Superior without sitting down. Mind you, she never offered me a chair. Anyway, she read the note, looked at me, read it again and said, 'I don't know. I just don't know'. Then she said 'Wait', left her seat behind the desk and walked out. All the while I was still standing there. I stared at the white walls of the plain room. Just two chairs and a desk. A large wooden cross with Christ hung on one of the walls. I had just walked over to examine it more closely, and she came back accompanied by a young nun. 'This is Sister Bernadette. She was with a party of her sisters searching for wood outside the convent when the planes hit Hildesheim. They watched a plane being hit by anti-aircraft guns, the plane spun out of control and some airmen descended by parachute. Most sisters dropped the wood they had gathered and ran back. However, Sister Bernadette seems to have trouble following orders and went to investigate.' Sister Francisca told me. The young Sister had her eyes focused on the floor all the time while Sister Francisca spoke. I felt so sorry for her. I almost said something, but only almost. Anyway, as it turns out, Sister Bernadette found two of them, one hanging from a tree upside down. His parachute had got caught in the branches. The other one nearby on the ground was not moving. Sister Bernadette hurried back to the convent, alerting Sister Francisca, who was not too pleased I gathered, from the way she spoke. It was, she said, 'Their Christian duty to help these unfortunate souls'. It took several nuns to carry both English airmen back on the stretchers. As soon as they had them settled, she sent for Brother Thomas. As far as she knows, Brother Thomas took them at night on a cart all the way to Riddagshausen Abbey, near Braunschweig. Whether they survived the long journey, she did not know."

Chapter 74

Garston, Liverpool

Dear Flo,

I hope you are alright and come back soon. It was so good to receive your letter, and it made me laugh when you told me the incident about that little dog chasing you down the lane and you having to hide in someone's house, only to be mistaken for a burglar. I am smiling now, just thinking about it. Our Dorothy is still sulking that you did not take her with you when you went. I think you will be in real trouble with her when you come back unless you have something in your luggage for her reminding her of Ballyshannon. I never imagined Ireland would have such an effect on her.

Guess what, you will not believe this one! Joseph came back from Germany on leave last week. He went straight to Kate's house! He thinks he's found William!!!!!!!!!!! I don't know all the details, only what Kate told me in her excitement. He is stationed in the town where he saw William being shot down. There, he met some GERMANS!!!!! He said one of the women he met speaks good English. With Joseph, it would be a woman who helps him!! Anyway, this woman knew somebody in the hospital there and then they checked at their local convent. How that came about I do not remember. After that, they went to a town called Brunswick, I think that's what she said the town was called. There were two of them at the beginning. Two RAF men, I mean. One of them died on the way there. A monk, oh, yes I forgot in Brunswick they had to go to an abbey. The monk there gave Joseph the dog tag from the RAF man who died and was buried there. They let Joseph see the grave they had dug. That was good of them to bury him at the abbey! What do you think? Anyway the ID was NOT William's. I hope I remember this right. The second man was badly injured, and the monks thought if they treated him themselves he would not survive. Apparently, the hospital there was not badly damaged. Thank God for that I can only say. The monk later tried to find out what happened to him and was told he had recovered they had no choice but to hand him over to the authorities who transported him to a POW camp somewhere near Berlin. I think there is a sort of agreement between countries at war that when you capture your enemy, you must treat them well and keep them. Fancy me using the word enemy when I speak about our William. Joseph gave the dog tag to the officer in charge at the garrison and here comes the GOOD news. All airmen on that mission have now been accounted for, besides William. So it has to be William, right?

Joseph has gone back to Germany now. Our Kate believes there is a German woman over there he fancies.

By the way, the other day George was stopped by somebody from the Corporation when he went past your house and had a quick check that everything was alright. This bloke asked whether you are coming back soon to live there. Otherwise, they want to use the house for another family. George reminded him, I don't think very politely, that all your payments are up to date, so what is he talking about. The bloke said 'be that as it may'. Yes, those were the exact words what he used, 'be that as it may' does George not know that there is a housing shortage and it does not do to have good houses standing empty. We have now been informed officially, he added, and we better have an answer for him soon. Flo, I think this is serious, so you have to tell me whether you are coming back and when.

Bob had his operation and Peg said he is doing well. But she looked really worried when she told me. They are trying a new drug on him now, called, I know I spell this incorrectly, Cemotherapie, something like that. It is quite a new idea, our Peg said. They still have not said anything about it to the Australian High Commission, nor have they told their children. They don't want to 'rock the boat,' she said.

Well, Flo, I will close now, I can go via the post office on my way to clean the Co-op. You know I miss you terrible, so I don't have to say that.

Love from everybody here, especially from me.

Annie

Chapter 75

January 1947

'Click'. Annie closed the two locks on the small brown suitcase and placed it back underneath the bed. Derek's cardigan, the one he never had a chance to wear, held in her hand. She let the case stick out just a little. She glimpsed at it when she went to bed. That was her way to make sure Derek stayed part of her family. Her little boy. Some of the things, which belonged to him, she would never hand down. She was sure of that. Annie would say goodnight to him before she pulled the blanket over her freezing body.

George and the children should be home soon. The children had a note for their teachers, and Grace had gone to get some flowers from the greengrocer at Vineyard Street. Flo went to Liverpool Lime Street Station. The train from London should have arrived by now. It was strange that Flo had to take a placard with their names on it. How else would they recognise her after all those years? Annie does not remember when Peg decided to tell her children. A telegram arrived from Perth saying that the children were boarding a ship to come back home. There was no time for Peg to protest. By the time she received it, the children had started their long journey. She knew they were entitled to their free trip back home, and there was nothing she could do. Soon, she would be holding her children in her arms. Bob had smiled at her when she told him but soon drifted back off to sleep. This new treatment they were trying out made him very sick and tired.

Now it was up to Flo to greet them with the news. The

butcher, who lived at Stamfordham Drive and who had helped them before, sprang into action again. He insisted he would drive Flo down into Liverpool himself and wait for her to find the children. Who knows how much luggage they'll bring back, he reasoned.

"Mam, I am home." David kicked his shoes off and dropped his gloves and scarf on to the floor outside the kitchen.

"David, don't just leave them there." Annie was tired, and all energy seemed to have drained from her during the last few weeks. The pains on her left side kept coming back, and she was out of breath most of the time.

"Mam, they are all wet."

"David, be a good boy and put them over the drying rack in front of the fire in the sitting room. At least until your dad gets here."

David walked over to his mother. She still sat on the bed. "Mam, are you alright?"

"Yes, my boy, just come and help your mam, will you?"

"Mam, can I get you something, can I make you a cup of tea? That's what you always say when somebody doesn't feel well, right?"

"Do you know how to do that?"

"I do." David walked back into the hall ready to go into the kitchen but not before turning round and announcing, "The teacher said I don't need to come back to school this week."

Annie felt dizzy and fell backwards on to the pillow. I might as well have a rest while I can. Tomorrow is going to be a difficult day, she thought.

"Here is your tea, Mam. See, I can do it." David proudly carried his mam's best cup and saucer, having spilled only very little. "Shall I open the box of biscuits?" he asked hopefully.

"You know they are for tomorrow, but go on, let's have

a biscuit." David was back in the kitchen before his mam could change her mind. "Mam, where is Alfie?" He sat on the bed next to his mother with his head against the headrest.

"He is downstairs playing with Audrey's little boy."

"There is somebody at the front door, maybe it is him. Shall I have a look?"

"Yes, see who it is."

"It's Aunty Flo, Mam! Aunty Flo, we are in my mam's bedroom having tea."

"Is there enough for me, young man?"

"I get you one. Mam, can Aunty Flo have a biscuit as well?"

"Just bring them all, David."

"Really?"

"How did it go, Flo?" Annie looked at her friend.

"Not good, they took it badly. Honestly I could not wait to drop them off at Peg's and leave."

Chapter 76

Dorothy pushed Alfie in his pushchair and David had placed his hand on to the side of it. For once, David did not speak or lark about. He did not even protest this morning when it was Grace who gave him a good scrub down with only lukewarm water. He looked round towards his mam. Both his mam and his dad were carrying a heavy basket between them. Its contents were for later on, his mam had told him. Jeffrey had gone ahead; Aunty Peg had asked him to come early. They could do with an extra pair of hands, she had said. Flo and Grace were walking behind his mam and dad.

"Dorothy," he whispered."

"What?"

"This jumper is really itchy."

"David, for goodness sake, is that all you have to worry about?"

"But it is."

"David, you better don't ruin it, our mam borrowed it and we have to give it back tonight, remember?"

"Dorothy?"

"What now?"

"Do you remember our cousins?"

"David, I hardly remember you, now how would I remember our cousins."

"You two stop arguing."

"See, now you made our dad tell us off. Mam, can David walk with you?"

"Yes, can I?"

David did not wait for a reply and was at his mam's side before his dad said no.

"Mam?"

"Yes, David."

"Was that Derek's cardigan Alfie is wearing?"

"Yes, it was."

"Did I ever wear it when I was little?"

"That is it, David, one more word from you and you are going back home."

George had stopped and put the basket down for a minute. He had heard Annie's laboured breathing and worried that she had caught one of those bugs going round at the moment.

"Come on, George, I'll help you with that." Flo had stepped forward and bent down to pick up the basket, receiving a thankful look from Annie in return.

"We are nearly there, anyway."

They all stopped at the end of Stamfordham Drive. The black hearse stood outside Peg's house. Shauna and Matthew spotted them and slowly walked towards them. David was just going to run off to greet them, but his mam pulled him back by his arm.

"Not today, David." He looked up and realised that tears were forming in his mam's eyes. He had only ever seen his mam crying once before, and that was when Dorothy got back from Ireland. She had told him then that those were tears of joy. But his mam's eyes did not look joyful now.

"We'll take that, Uncle George," Matthew greeted them. "It is just in time to go into the butcher's van to be taken down to the working men's club. We'll go there later because it is not that far to walk."

"Come with us, David?"

"Can I, Mam?"

"We have to wait outside until it is time to leave, our mam said so," Shauna said.

"Why do we have to wait outside?" David asked when they were out of earshot.

"Uncle Bob is still inside."

"Is he really?"

"Yes and our dad and Uncle Paddy are sitting next to him. Our mam says they are paying their last respects."

"Did you know that Uncle Paddy is moving back here and will stay with Aunty Peg for a while?"

"Is he?"

"Yes, he and our dad have spent a lot of time together since our dad got back from Germany. Our mam says, she thinks there must be a special bond between people who survived the war."

"It's good your dad came back, isn't it?" said David.

"Yes, it's great."

Peg's front door opened. The undertakers carried a light brown coffin on their shoulders followed by a sombre group of people dressed in black.

The first man in the group turned round and looked at the children. David and Matthew were still holding the basket. The man gave a small wave. David recognised him and could not contain himself any longer. He let the basket go and ran towards the man.

"Uncle William!" David landed in William's arms.

Epilogue

Annie, George and their children moved into Stamfordham Drive in 1951 and lived next door to her sisters, Peg and Kate.

Peg and her children stayed in England and rebuilt their lives without Bob.

Kate and William slowly came to terms with what had happened to him. The head injury he sustained during his parachute descent meant he found it difficult to re-adjust and concentrate on regular work, especially in the beginning. Paddy trained to be a social worker, and with his help William got stronger.

Flo and Annie remained close friends. Flo remarried, her new husband was the caretaker of the wash house she had met after the war.

Maria's husband Egon was one of the first POWs to be released from England and continued his work at the hospital in Hildesheim. In the mid-1950s Maria and Egon moved their family to England and lived in Walton-on-Thames, Surrey.

Joseph stayed in Germany. Hilde and Joseph's daughter was born in August 1948. Joseph insisted they call her Elisabeth.

And their daughter Elisabeth? Elisabeth met David, they married and now live in the south of England, across the Solent, near the Isle of Wight.

The Night I Danced with Rommel

Prologue

14 October 1944 – Hildesheim, Germany

"Why do people die, Mama?" I went over to where he was standing and put my arms around him. Klaus pushed me away. "The man pappa works for, has he really died?"

How could I explain the horror of it all to a seven-year-old boy, but I could not lie to him.

"Yes, I think the man your Pappa works for, Field Marshal Rommel, he is dead."

But why, Mama? Why do people die?"

"I think sometimes God wants them to come and live with him." I hoped this would help him to understand.

"But doesn't God want everybody to come and live with him?"

"Yes he does, but special people, he might want those to live with him earlier and that is when God has to make a quick decision, you see?"

"You mean, like when he wanted Inge to come and live with him, even though we wanted Inge to stay here with us?"

"Yes, Klaus, just like it was with Inge." I had to look away. I did not want him to realise how hard it was not to cry.

"But my pappa, my pappa, he will come home," he decided and went back into the kitchen to join the other children.

Coming soon...

Cuckoo Clock

Chapter 1

9 November 1938 – Hildesheim, Germany

Esther tried to listen for her father in the room next to hers. But any noise in the house was drowned out by the riots outside.

"Father we have to hurry. Just take a few things, as we discussed. Hurry, Father."

She was not surprised that she did not receive a reply. Her father was a proud man. Even the love for his only child could not persuade him to accept defeat.

"I think you are panicking for nothing," he said, putting his head round the door.

"Our family has been a respected member of this community for centuries. Why do you think anything would happen to us now?"

"Father, we don't have the time to discuss it again. Please just do as I ask."

"No, I made up my mind, I am not leaving. You can, if you want to, but I still believe in humanity. I am staying here. This is our home."

Esther sighed and put the woollen coat down. She was glad she had bought it last year when things were still a little easier. It was good quality and she was an excellent seamstress. A trade she had learned from her mother, before she was so cruelly taken from them. She could see her mother standing there now in front of her. It was a trick she had learned all those years ago. She would not go to sleep at night until she had concentrated hard enough to make her mother appear at the end of the bed. She knew it was not real, but it gave her great comfort and strength. Her mother had meant well during the few years they had spent together. From her she learned her independence and not to take people at face value. Esther had listened carefully to all the advice her mother gave her every time Esther's father was out at his workshop. "You are being too strict with our girl, Devora," he used to scold her. "Mordechai, these are uncertain times," was her reply every time. In the end he gave up and winked at Esther and rolled his eyes upwards, then looking at her mother. Esther used to smile at him politely but secretly she sided with her mother instead of with her ever-optimistic father. "Don't fill our girl's head with your nonsense when I am out Devora, you hear," he said most mornings.

"I am nearly done here and then I am helping you, Father. Only one small case each, remember? We both can take a rucksack as well with some provisions. Here, I finished your jacket, now give me your coat."

He came back and threw it on her bed. His coat was not as heavy as her own, but it would have to do. She was glad that vanity did not overtake her common sense when she got hers. Yes, the fur coat was very tempting indeed and her friend would not understand why she did not buy that one instead. After all, it is a bargain, she insisted. Esther just had this feeling. Maybe it was her mother looking down at her.

"I like this one," she lied. "I love how it feels and look at the big collar."

What she really liked about it was the heavy lining. A good place to hide things in. "It's like a man's coat and look, it is far too long. You almost disappear in it," her friend went on.

Finished! She lifted the coat off the bed several times, as

if she was weighing it. After that she felt around the collar, followed by brushing her hands over the lining all the way to the bottom of the coat. Not bad. Her father's jacket had seemed less obvious. We might just get away with it but his coat will be a problem. Well, she sighed again, it's the only one he's got and we don't have much more left anyway.

Esther took her mother's gold necklace and matching bracelet. The stones already removed. Now just her rings and she was done.

Her father came back into her room and saw his gold pocket watch still untouched on the blanket. "What about my watch?"

"No, you take it and put it in your waistcoat pocket as usual."

"But why, surely it would be the first thing to lose."

"Father, we can't travel anywhere without any jewellery. Nobody would believe us and then they would carry out a proper search. Is that what you want?"

Mordechai had no intention to agree with his daughter. My Esther thinks I am a fool, he thought. Better that way. There was one thing he was not going to leave behind and he had packed it in the bottom of his rucksack. It was quite bulky and heavy and he only had a little space for provisions on top. Unless she insisted he unpack and show her everything he planned to take, there would be no way she would find out until it was too late.

They opened their front door. The sun was rising to her east. Esther looked up. No clouds but smoke obscured her view. It could have been a wonderful day today, she thought. Esther did not want to look to her left but temptation was stronger. The synagogue was still smouldering. There were broken windows in the houses opposite. Open doors and items of china smashed on to the street. The doors which were closed had red swastikas crudely painted on them.

"Come on, Father, it is time for us to leave."

The Kessler Strasse, seemed deserted, even so they kept their heads down and tried to go as fast as Mordechai could manage. Esther had been worried about him for some time and looked at him now. His once straight frame seemed to have shrunk and stooped, as if all his fighting spirit had left him. Maybe we should have left sooner. She took her free hand and placed it into his. Something she had not done since she was a small girl. He turned round and she saw his grateful look as he felt his hand taken in a firm grip.

Walking down the main shopping street they carefully stepped over broken glass from smashed store windows. Esther glanced into some of them. The stores were looted. Frau Neuberger was outside her toyshop near the market square sweeping glass from one corner into the other without much purpose. She looked at them with a blank expression, bent her head down and carried on. Mordechai pulled away and was going to speak with her. Esther held on to her father, preventing him going, and shook her head.

Further down the road they saw people queuing at the station long before they reached it. Wordlessly they joined the queue. Soon other people stood behind them. The queue was not moving. Soldiers in SS uniforms marched up and down, assisted by some young boys in Hitler Youth uniforms.

"Papers!" the soldiers barked.

Esther saw three women with a pushchair and children walking at the hand of their mothers. She recognised Maria, Egon's wife. He was one of the doctors she worked with at the hospital. Maria had spotted her and tried to come over but was being stopped by one of the pimply youths.

The women next to Maria shouted at the boy. He looked at her, his face bright red and let Maria pass.

"Esther, where are you going?"

"Maria, it is no longer safe for us here. They have arrested most of the men this morning, including my husband. I had to promise him that I would try and leave with my father today. He gave me your brother's address. I will be in touch with him. God bless you, Maria."

Lightning Source UK Ltd.
Milton Keynes UK
UKHW040639200921
390889UK00001B/85